Claiming the Billionaire

T0364278

Also by JM Stewart

Bidding on the Billionaire
Winning the Billionaire
Bargaining for the Billionaire

Claiming the Billionaire

JM STEWART

FOREVER
YOURS

New York   Boston

Copyright © 2017 by JM Stewart
Excerpt from *Bidding on the Billionaire* copyright © 2016 by JM Stewart
Cover design by Elizabeth Turner
Cover copyright © 2017 by Hachette Book Group, Inc.

Forever Yours
Hachette Book Group
1290 Avenue of the Americas
New York, NY 10104
forever-romance.com
twitter.com/foreverromance

First Edition: January 2017

Forever Yours is an imprint of Grand Central Publishing.
The Forever Yours name and logo are trademarks of Hachette Book Group, Inc.

The Hachette Speakers Bureau provides a wide range of authors for speaking events. To find out more, go to www.hachettespeakersbureau.com or call (866) 376-6591.

ISBN 978-1-4555-9227-2 (ebook edition)
ISBN 978-1-4555-9228-9 (print on demand edition)

Claiming the Billionaire

Chapter One

Cassie, honey, are you sitting down?"

Phone in one hand, pitcher of water in the other, Cassandra Stephanopoulos halted dead center of her kitchen. The coffee she'd been in the process of making went forgotten as ice skittered down her spine, plunking hard and cold in her belly and awakening her sleepy senses. Every bit of bad news she'd ever received seemed to come off the heels of a line like that.

Any other day, she wouldn't have picked up her phone before she'd had a much needed morning dose of caffeine. Things like talking coherently simply didn't happen before coffee. She'd glanced at the screen, though. Who the hell would call her so early? Her girls and her best friend, Grayson, all knew she wasn't a morning person.

However, at seeing Marilyn Benson's number, she'd snatched her phone off the counter. Marilyn was Tyler's mother. His family was her only connection to him now. It was a tiny, stupid little scrap to hold on to. It wouldn't bring him back, but she needed the connection like she needed oxygen.

More to the point, Marilyn had only called her this early twice: the first time to tell her Tyler had gone missing. The second…to tell her they'd called off the search for him. All of which now had Cassie's mind racing with horrible possibilities. Her hands began to shake, sending the cold water sloshing over the rim of the full pitcher and onto her bare toes.

She deposited the pitcher on the nearest counter, pinched the bridge of her nose, and forced herself to count to three before answering. She would *not* allow the panic slithering up her spine to take root. "Is everything okay? Are Dean and the girls all right?"

Tyler's older brother, Dean, and his wife, Kathy, had two gorgeous little girls with the biggest blue eyes Cassie had ever seen. Every time she saw them, they made her chest ache, because she always wondered. If Tyler had lived and she hadn't taken the coward's way out by turning down his proposal, would their kids have inherited those eyes as well?

"Sweetie, I have something to tell you. I wanted you to know before it ends up on the news."

Before it ended up on the news? Cassie's stomach sank into her toes. Now she knew it was bad. She reached out to grip the edge of a nearby counter and swallowed past the thick paste in her throat. "My stomach's in knots. Whatever it is, just tell me. Please."

On the other end of the line, Marilyn drew a shaky breath. "Sweetie, Tyler's alive."

Marilyn's voice came out barely above a whisper, but she might as well have shouted the words. Everything inside Cassie skidded to a halt. She stared out the long row of windows on the other side of her penthouse apartment. Despite it being January in Seattle, the skies were clear blue. The beauty somehow added a surreal quality to the moment. How many times had she longed for this exact phone call? Surely she was only dreaming…

"Come again?"

Marilyn laughed, the sound of someone so relieved they were beside themselves. "He's alive. I just spoke with him. He sounds a little shaky, to be honest, but he's alive. Apparently, he was held captive somewhere in Iraq. I'm afraid I don't know the whole story yet, but oh, sweetie, he's coming home."

Marilyn continued to ramble, her voice a giddy, half-delirious murmur on the other end of the line, but the actual words didn't register. The impact of the news struck Cassie like an arrow, piercing her heart. She sagged back against the kitchen counter, staring at everything and nothing, as tears rushed over her, bringing with them a profound sense of relief.

Tyler was alive.

* * *

Cassie bebopped to the tune playing in her right ear as she made her way down the hotel corridor. The long hallway stood empty, save a few other last-minute arrivals. Grayson, her long-time best friend, and his new wife, Maddie, walked a couple steps behind, their gaits more casual than Cassie's buoyant stride. It was rude to listen to music in the presence of friends, but as newlyweds, Maddie and Gray had gone off in a world of their own, and Cassie needed the upbeat tune to bolster her mood. Maybe if she forced herself to be cheerful, she'd eventually feel it.

She couldn't believe she'd let Gray talk her into this. She didn't want to be here. No, she'd rather be alone in her penthouse with a fifth of scotch, getting so drunk she couldn't remember her name. A week had passed since Marilyn had called to tell her Tyler was alive. Marilyn had been right. Every news channel was talking about it. Somehow he'd not only managed to survive being captured by insurgents, but he'd also gotten himself home. To say she was relieved would be the understatement of the century.

Except he hadn't come to see her. He'd been home for seven days now and he hadn't so much as called her. But why would he? After the way they'd left things, the things they'd said to each other, she certainly wouldn't come to see her either.

She wasn't even sure she wanted him to. It wasn't fair to want to see him, really. Nothing had changed for her. Tyler would be a soldier until he died. It was who he was. And she still couldn't risk losing another person she loved. She'd lost her brother in Iraq five years ago…after losing their mother five years before that. Their family hadn't been the same since Nick's death. Her *baba* had shut her out, lost to his grief. She couldn't, wouldn't, go through that again, lose one more person.

She couldn't deny, though, that it still hurt. That she still had an overpowering need to see him. Her heart wouldn't fully trust that he really was alive until she saw him with her own two eyes.

Exactly why she'd allowed Gray to drag her to this auction. Because clearly seeing him again wasn't going to happen, and she desperately needed a distraction.

When the too-familiar pain began to wrap itself around her chest again, Cassie refocused on the upbeat music and paused to shimmy out the last strains of the song. She'd have fun tonight if it killed her.

Behind her, Gray chuckled. "I'm glad to see you're in a good mood tonight, Cassie. I thought you'd be pissed when I showed up earlier. I know you didn't really want to participate in this auction."

She pulled out the earbud and looked down at her phone, closing the music app.

"You're lucky. I've heard about these shindigs from a few friends. If I'm lucky, I'll end up with two of Christina's hotties." She shot a wink over her shoulder. "They can make me a Cassie sandwich."

Okay, so that wasn't really what she wanted. She'd intended to spend tonight alone, wallowing in her self-pity, but Gray had waylaid those plans. He'd shown up at her apartment two hours ago, demanded she get dressed, and dragged her out to his car. He hadn't told her where they were headed until they were halfway here.

Cassie had known Christina McKenzie, now apparently Christina Blake, in high school. Christina ran a charity auction that had become famous over the last few years. This year, she'd turned the tables a bit. Instead of bachelors, they were auctioning the ladies. Gray had talked her into signing up as one of the bachelorettes. Any other time, this would have been exactly her style. An evening with a potentially hot guy? Yeah, she'd have been all over that. Tonight all she really wanted was a pint of Ben & Jerry's and a really big spoon.

Gray rolled his eyes as he came to a stop beside her. "Some things haven't changed, I see."

"Actually, I've decided you're right, Gray. This is exactly the distraction I need tonight. Besides, you only live once." She playfully nudged him with an elbow. "You should have volunteered Maddie. You can make a Maddie sandwich."

"I don't share." Gray glared at her, but the corners of his mouth twitched with his effort to hold back a grin.

Okay, so it wasn't nice to tease him, but Grayson Lockwood had been her best friend since high school. Since that tenth-grade English class she'd only passed because he'd taken pity on her. They teased each other as easily as they confided in each other. Besides, it's what he got for storming her apartment.

Luckily for her, the gleam in Maddie's eyes told her she'd gotten the joke. Maddie winked, covered her mouth, and let out a girlish giggle. Cassie bit the inside of her cheek to keep from laughing. She and Maddie might have had a rocky start, but they were becoming fast friends. Maddie had a wicked sense of humor and a heart of gold. She also made Gray happy.

Gray jerked his gaze to his wife. "And what are *you* laughing at?"

Maddie blinked up at him, innocence personified. "What? I kind of like the idea. Didn't you say you wanted to try something different?"

Gray turned his head, shooting Cassie a glare. "Touché, Cassandra. Touché. Consider us even now." He jerked his gaze back to Maddie. "You, however, I can spank."

When he backed Maddie against the nearest wall and set his hands on either side of her head, Cassie turned away from the newlyweds. She was damn happy for them. She really was. After a long, painful road that had nearly taken Maddie and Gray away from each other and the dangerous childhood he'd endured, Gray deserved to be happy. She needed him to be.

Seeing them together, though, made her chest ache. She'd had that once, and every time they nuzzled each other, she was reminded of how much she missed it.

"Don't take too long. You guys only have five minutes." Cassie shot a sassy wink over her shoulder and turned, striding for the ballroom entrance at the end of the hall.

She came to a stop inside and took a moment to gather herself. She'd only get through tonight by smiling and pretending life was a party. If luck found her, maybe she'd fake herself into believing her chest wasn't caving in.

Inside, the place was more men than women, every one of them dressed to the nines. The men gorgeous and debonair in their black tuxes, the women regal and glowing in their finest gowns and jewels. Each face lit up with the promise of the evening. A feeling she wished she shared. The whole evening exhausted her. She wasn't in the mood to put on the act tonight.

"Don't think I didn't see what you did back there."

Gray's deep voice sounded behind her seconds before his hand settled on her shoulder, warm and heavy and supportive.

Cassie darted a glance at him. "Shouldn't you be whisking Maddie off to a dark corner somewhere?"

As if on cue, Maddie stepped up beside Gray.

"I'm going to go find Christina and say hello." Maddie lifted onto her toes, kissed him softly, and turned to Cassie. She took one of Cassie's hands, offering a sympathetic smile. "All kidding aside, I'm glad you're here. Don't be too mad at him. This part was my idea. I hated the thought of you sitting home alone, feeling miserable, so I told Gray to go over and get you. Hannah always did that for me, those three years Gray and I were apart. Forced me to get up, to live. It was hard, but she was right."

She'd come to adore Maddie. Turned out, they had a lot in common. They both had pasts they regretted, and like Cassie, Maddie tended to put on a front, to avoid feeling things. More to the point, what Maddie had gone through with Gray meant she understood the moment Cassie had arrived at—knowing she needed to move on but not knowing how.

Cassie plastered on the best smile she could muster.

"Thank you. I'm not mad. I'm just not sure I'm up for this."

Maddie squeezed her fingers. "Smile like it's the best night of your life. Besides, whoever it is you end up with, you're only required a single date. At the very least, he'll keep your mind off your heart."

Cassie watched Maddie's fiery hair disappear into the crowd before glancing at Gray. "I really like her. She's good for you."

She had to admit, she was grateful for a moment alone with him. Only with Gray did she feel comfortable letting down her walls. Even her father put pressure on her to be someone else. Someone more perfect. With her *baba*, nothing she did was ever enough. *"When are you going to get serious, Cassandra? You can't play like a child all your life. I'm not going to be around forever. Who will take over the restaurants when I die?"* Her father had said the words so many times she could hear his Greek accent echo in her head even now.

She was her father's biggest disappointment. He and her mother had opened Ariana's Greek Café before she and her brother, Nick, were born. Authentic Greek cuisine, with recipes that had been passed down for generations. She and Nick had been raised in those restaurants and Daddy insisted they learn the business, to take over when he and Mom could no longer run them. Now that they'd lost her mother to that car accident and Nick to the war, the heavy burden had fallen to her. Cassie wasn't a restaurateur. She designed jewelry, custom-made pieces. She had the soul of an artist. Creations by Cassie was doing better than ever. A handful of large stores had even commissioned pieces. All of which displeased her father no end.

Gray, though, always accepted her as she was, broken, crabby bits and all.

Gray pulled her against his side. "Maddie likes you, too. I warned her you probably wouldn't be yourself tonight."

"I appreciate it. Tell her I said thanks. I hope she knows it isn't personal." Cassie scanned the crowd again and sighed. "Remind me again why I'm here?"

"Because she's right. You sitting at home crying your eyes out doesn't do you any good. You being one of the bachelorettes gives you a purpose, something to do. Besides, raccoon eyes aren't a good look on you."

He winked, and she let out a watery laugh, but staring into the room, the weight of the entire evening pressed down on her. "I don't know how to let him go, Gray. I tried for three years. I want to have fun tonight, but I'm not sure I can. It's killing me that he hasn't even called me."

Nor did she think she deserved the happiness she coveted. The time she saw Tyler, she'd told him she'd used him, but she'd lied through her teeth. He was deploying, and she couldn't lose another person she loved.

Except the joke had been on her. She'd waited anyway, had worried anyway, and when Tyler hadn't come home, the bottom had dropped out of her world. His death had left her struggling. To move on. To release the guilt caught in her chest. To live.

She released the memory and peered up at Grayson. "His last memories of us were me telling him he was nothing but my latest boy toy. I can't forgive myself for that. Clearly, he can't either."

"Let me talk to Christina." Grayson released her shoulders and turned to face her. "I'm willing to bet she'd know the perfect guy to fix you up with. If I know her, she knows everyone here personally. I bet she can fix you up with someone who won't expect anything from you."

Cassie rolled her eyes. "That's pathetic. I can get my own dates."

One dark brow lifted in challenge. "Then why aren't you?"

"Point taken." Six months ago, when she'd stood as his "best woman" at his wedding, she'd come to a realization. Watching Gray profess to love, honor, and cherish Maddie for the rest of his life had been an honest moment for her. She couldn't deny that, deep down, she wanted what they'd found. The happily-ever-after.

She'd decided that day to stop living a lie. Her jewelry had borne the brunt of her insomnia. Some of her best work had taken shape at one in the morning, often fueled by heartache. Apparently, sleepless nights and lack of sex were good muses.

Tonight, she needed her carefree side or she wouldn't make it to morning without curling up into a sobbing mess. She was glad Tyler was alive. The knowledge eased a wound in her soul. A world without him in it didn't make sense. Except she now had to face losing him a second time.

She turned her head to search the ballroom, stopping when she found her target. "I see the bar. I'm going to get a drink before this starts. A strong one."

Gray laid a hand on her shoulder. "We'll be sitting toward the middle. They should be starting soon."

She reached back, settling her hand over his in return. "Thanks. I won't be long."

Approaching the bar, the hunky blond behind the counter flashed a thousand-watter and rested his hands on the surface. She didn't miss the appreciative gleam in his eyes as his gaze swept over her. "What can I get you, sweetheart?"

Momentarily distracted, she smiled in return. His grin could charm the panties off even the coldest woman, and with muscles on top of muscles, he looked like he could be one of Christina's bachelors. He'd no doubt been hired for that reason.

Deciding to grab the evening by its ears, to not let the pain suck her under, she pulled her "bad girl without a conscience" out of her closet. She leaned on the bar, giving Mr. Muscles the once-over, along with a view of her cleavage. "Give me a Screaming Orgasm."

Okay, so she'd rather have two fingers of scotch, but flirting with Mr. Muscles over there was exactly what the doctor prescribed.

Luckily for her, he took her sassy order with good humor. He grinned, one corner of his mouth hitching higher than the other, and pulled out a tumbler. He filled it with ice, added equal parts vodka, Irish cream, and coffee liqueur, and winked at her as he pushed the drink across the counter. "I get off at ten. For now, this'll have to do."

Cassie laughed. Yup. He'd definitely been hired for a purpose. No doubt he sold more liquor on his flirtatious smile alone. "You should be careful with lines like that. A lesser woman might take you up on it."

He leaned his elbows on the bar, his grin widening. "Who says it was a line?"

She laughed again and dug in her purse, pulled out a hundred-dollar bill, and stuffed it into the tip jar on the counter. "Honey, you just made my night."

Someone tapped the microphone. "Pardon the interruption, everyone. Can I have the ladies onstage please? We'll begin in a few minutes."

"Oops, that's me." She picked up her drink off the counter and saluted him before tipping the contents into her mouth. It slid smooth and creamy down her throat, hitting her belly and warming her from the inside. It didn't thaw the ice around her heart, but it went a long way. She winked at Mr. Muscles. "Bachelorette number one."

Somewhat bolstered, she made her way onto the small stage, taking her place at the head of the line of women. Busy finding their seats, the crowd beyond the stage wove their way through the rows of gray folding chairs. She had to hand it to them. The men were subtle, respectful. A group of women getting ready to outbid each other over hunky bachelors would have been a whole lot more raucous. Maddie, who'd attended the last three, had told her as much.

As it turned out, Gray and Maddie were seated at the end of a row in the center of it all. He caught her eye and gave her a thumbs-up. Cassie smiled in return. Yeah, she could do this.

Christina stepped up to the podium, back straight, hands

resting on the wooden surface. "Thank you all for coming tonight. Welcome to the fifth annual auction for breast cancer research. Of course, we're all here for the same reason. To fight this disease. Breast cancer has claimed too many women in my family. I know some of you here tonight are survivors. I say we fight this disease with a little style. Now, every year since its inception, I've gathered Seattle's finest bachelors. This year, I thought the men deserved a little treat. "

Applause erupted through the ballroom. Several whoops came from various parts of the room. Christina laughed and waved her hands to quiet the crowd.

"All right, gentlemen. Allow me to introduce our first bachelorette, miss Cassandra Stephanopoulos."

At hearing her name, Cassie drew a deep breath, straightened her shoulders, and moved toward the podium. Drawing her inner vixen around her, she plastered on her flirtiest smile and put a little extra swing in her hips. Applause once again erupted around the room. From somewhere in the back, a wolf whistle pierced the air, though the lights pointed at the stage made seeing where it had come from near impossible.

Christina turned to wink at her as she approached the podium. "It appears you already have fans."

Cassie laughed and took a bow. "Thank you. I'll be here all night."

"Gentlemen, a little about Cassie. Her father owns and runs the chain of Greek restaurants, Ariana's Greek Café. She paints and designs custom jewelry. Her shop, Creations by Cassie, sits a few blocks from here. In fact, for any ladies in attendance, she designed the necklace I'm wearing. When asked, she said she likens herself to a sorority girl—she's just out to have a little fun." Christina looked up from her cards, winking at the audience. "But don't get any ideas, guys. Her best friend is the big guy in the fifth row."

Gray stood, humor lacing his tone as he turned his head, addressing the crowd around him. "Consider me her personal bouncer."

When he bowed, Cassie playfully rolled her eyes. The crowd laughed.

Christina let out a soft laugh as well. "Actually, Cassie told me she thinks life is too short to be too serious. Isn't that right, Cassie?"

Cassie forced herself to smile and nod, but her heart ached. Thinking she'd lost Tyler, on top of losing her mother and her brother, had taught her something. "I fully intend to enjoy the life I have. Live it to the fullest. Good food, good wine, good friends."

Christina wrapped an arm around her, giving her a gentle, reassuring hug, before turning back to the crowd. Clearly Gray had filled her in. "All right, shall we start the bidding?"

More applause came from the crowd as Christina stepped back and the auctioneer took her place at the podium. "All right, gentlemen, let's start the bidding at ten thousand…"

Several minutes passed as bids ping-ponged around the room, each one higher than the last.

"One hundred thousand," a man's voice called out from the back of the long room.

Cassie froze.

She knew that voice. She'd know it in the dead of night, in the darkest cave.

The familiar sound of it skittered down her spine, and her playful smile melted. Her hands shook at her sides. Heart hammering, she shielded her eyes, squinting against the bright lights aimed at the stage, and searched the crowd for the face to go with the voice. Even while she searched, rational thought warred with the pain still pounding around in her chest. It couldn't be Tyler. He wouldn't have come to see her. She'd hurt him too much, had looked him right in the eye and told him he meant nothing to her beyond sex. And then sent him off to die.

The room fell silent, tension rising over the space.

Christina's hand slid over her shoulder, her voice warm and low in Cassie's ear. "You're three shades of white, honey. Are you all right?"

Cassie's blood roared in her ears, pounding so hard the room began to spin, but she forced herself to smile and glanced at Christina. "I'm fine. The voice just spooked me. Sounded like someone I know."

It had to be a trick of the room. The high ceilings made the noise echo. Combined with her grief, her ears clearly played tricks on her. She was hearing things, that's all.

Christina didn't look convinced. "Are you sure?"

Cassie nodded. "I'm fine. Continue, please. I'm sorry for the interruption."

Christina smiled and the auctioneer started the bidding again. As the bids once again ping-ponged around the room, the man in back, whose voice had spooked her, countered every bid. He didn't say anything else but raised his bidding number repeatedly. Several more minutes passed; as the bids rose higher, the number of men participating dwindling to two. Finally, when the numbers reached four hundred thousand, the second bidder bowed out.

"Sold. To the gentleman in the back."

As the auctioneer's voice rang through the room, the man in the back strode toward the stage. Cassie held her breath. The closer he got, the louder her heartbeat pounded in her ears. He looked like Tyler. He had the same tall build and broad shoulders, the same dark hair, cropped close, per army regulation. She couldn't see the color of his eyes from this distance, though. Not to mention he looked thinner than Ty had been the last time she'd seen him. Ty had always been a big, burly guy, tall and thickly muscled. This guy was tall but lean, and he walked with a slight limp Tyler hadn't had.

When he came to a stop in front of the stage, head tipped back to peer up at her, her heart stopped altogether. Closer now, she could clearly see his eyes were blue.

Like Ty's.

Nausea swirled in her stomach, at war with the guilt, the part of her that wanted, needed, this man to be Tyler. She knew better, though…didn't she?

The room swayed as dizziness swept over her. This was wrong. This was all wrong.

She jerked her gaze to Christina. "Is this some sort of a joke?"

Christina shook her head, looking between Cassie to the

audience in helpless confusion. "I have no idea what's going on, sweetie, but I assure you I had nothing to do with whatever this is."

Cassie turned to look out over the audience, her heart hammering in her ears. Marilyn's phone call came rushing back to her. *"Tyler's alive."*

She'd been waiting for this moment. She'd heard Marilyn's words that day, a week ago now, but hadn't truly believed them. She needed to see him.

Out in the audience, Gray pushed to his feet and strode toward the stage, his long strides closing the distance in record time. Concern etched his face.

"This isn't real. It can't be." Cassie shook her head, watching Tyler's eyes, waiting for him to explain, to say…something.

Tyler opened and closed his mouth a few times, but long moments passed in aching silence as he stared at her with tired eyes rimmed in shadows. Finally, his throat bobbed as he swallowed. "I had to see you."

Before she could think or remember to breathe, Gray came to a stop in front of the stage. He turned to glare at Tyler. "It's fucking cruel to show up this way, man."

Tyler turned his head, glaring back. "Three years. Three fucking years sitting…" He shook his head, his face blanching, and straightened his shoulders. "I saw the commercial on TV an hour ago. So fucking sue me for needing to see her."

The sound of his voice washed over her, and hope and an almost surreal sense of joy expanded inside of her. How many times over the last three years had she imagined this moment? That he'd come home and she'd know he was safe. God, simply to know he was safe…And there he was, close enough to touch. Her whole body trembled with the overwhelming need to jump from the stage and hurl herself into his arms. For the simple luxury of feeling him real and solid and whole.

He'd come. He'd actually come to see her.

As shock receded, the memory of the last time she saw him filled her mind. So vivid and corporeal it might have been only yesterday. Tyler down on one knee, looking gorgeous in his uniform, a diamond ring in one hand and his heart in his eyes.

"Marry me, Cassie."

Her response jolted through her next. The shock. The breath-stealing fear of losing him that had clenched at her chest. She'd turned his proposal down flat. Had looked him right in the eye and told him she didn't love him.

The wall she'd put her pain behind three years ago cracked. Three years of grief flooded over her like a tidal wave, and a vise closed around her chest, threatening to pull her knees out from beneath her.

"I can't deal with this." Cassie stalked from the stage, moving as fast as she dared without resorting to running as she headed out of the ballroom. Head spinning, her stomach churning, she stalked the long hallway and jabbed the button for the elevator, her mind focused on her car in the parking lot. Home. She needed to go home. This whole night was a bad idea.

She only made it to her car, parked at the back of the quiet lot, before the pain refused to be held back any longer. The sobs she'd buried all these years broke free, and she sagged against the driver's side door of her Jag as the tears washed down her cheeks.

How long she stood there sobbing, she didn't know, but footsteps sounded on the pavement somewhere beyond her, echoing around the quiet lot. She sniffled, clutched her keys tightly in her hand, ready to fend off an attacker if need be, and turned her head. Tyler jogged in her direction, the backdrop of the streetlights illuminating him from behind. Like a goddamn angel from heaven. He came to a stop in front of her, his tall, broad form towering over her, his chest heaving.

His warm breaths misted in the cool night air, and one corner of his mouth curled upward. "You're not making this easy, babe."

His voice was still hauntingly familiar. She reached out a tentative hand, searching the face she'd know in the dark. Prominent cheekbones. A strong jaw. He'd lost weight. The planes and angles of his face had become more pronounced, his skin paler, eyes sunken and rimmed in shadow. He had a haunted look about him now. "Tell me I'm not dreaming, Ty."

"I'll do you one better." He cupped her face in the warmth of his palms, stared for a moment, stroking his thumbs over her cheeks before leaning down and capturing her lips. His mouth was warm and familiar, but it wasn't the passionate kiss she remembered. He kissed her softly at first before settling his mouth more firmly over hers. His fingers trembled as they stroked her face.

Lost in the moment, in the fantasy, she leaned into him. Any minute now she'd wake up, and he'd go *poof*, and she'd find herself alone in bed. Right then, though, it was the best damn kiss she'd had in a long time, and God help her, she lifted onto her toes to get more of him. If she was dreaming, she had every intention of milking it.

When she laid her palms against his chest, needing his warmth, to feel the solidness of his body, he flinched again and jerked back. Confusion flicked over his features before recognition settled in his gaze. He fisted his hands in her hair, pulling her back to him, and rested his forehead against hers. "Jesus, I missed you."

His words finally rooted her, and the last lingering threads of denial unraveled, dragging her back to reality faster than a bucket of ice water. This wasn't a dream, some fantasy her mind had conjured. He *was* real.

All of which sent her hope spiraling straight into her toes. Tyler wouldn't have said that to her. The last time she'd seen him, they'd fought. She'd said horrible things to him that day, then sent him off to die. Why the hell would he miss *her*? Why would he even want her after the way she'd treated him? *She* wouldn't.

Drawing strength from the pain threatening to swallow her, she braced her hands against his chest and forced herself to step away from him. Keys clutched in her hand, she pointed the fob in his direction and glared at him. "I don't know what the hell kind of game you're playing, Ty, but you made your point, okay? This isn't funny anymore."

His brow furrowed in confusion and he opened his

mouth, but she hit the key fob and climbed inside her car, slamming the door. She hit the button to start the engine, dropped the shifter into drive, and stomped on the gas pedal. She didn't breathe or blink or even dare to look back until he'd become little more than a fading speck behind her.

Chapter Two

Staff Sergeant Tyler Benson drummed his fingers on his leg as he stared at the door in front of him. Over three years had passed since he'd last stood in this spot, staring at this door. Three years, two months, and seven days to be exact.

Yet the private vestibule around him looked the same. Gray marble flooring and matching walls. A chair and an end table, of all things, as if someone would sit out there to wait. Though he knew damn well he had, on more than one occasion. The space came complete with a fancy chandelier above his head. Cassie insisted on only the best. For her, it was the penthouse.

They were oil and water, from two contrasting worlds. He'd come from what his mother had always referred to as honest roots. She'd raised him and his older brother, Dean, on her own, after their father's death. Over the years, Mom had had to work two jobs in order to make ends meet, and he'd gone into the army because he wanted to make her proud.

Cassie was that untouchable girl, but she'd hooked him from the first sassy comeback she'd tossed at him the night they'd officially met. God, she had spunk.

Sitting in that poor excuse for a prison cell in Iraq, waiting, day after day, to die, he'd thought about her a lot. He had too many regrets when it came to her. Too many unanswered questions. Had he only imagined she'd had feelings for him, too? Had he imagined the tender way she'd stroke his cheek? Or the fierce possessiveness of her embrace in the darkness of night?

He'd thought about the last night he saw her the most. He knew finding him at the auction wouldn't go over easy, but he had to see her. He needed to see the light in her eyes, her smile. Hell, simply to stand within the same space as her, if only to prove to himself he hadn't imagined her.

Drawing a deep breath, he squared his shoulders and forced himself to knock on the door. Restless anxiety had adrenaline firing through him, and Tyler turned and paced the tiny hallway. He'd endured three years in an Iraqi prison, had been shot, beaten, and starved, watched men he lived and fought with die in front of him. In awful ways. Yet somehow, the thought of seeing Cassie again had his heart jackhammering his ribs.

When grumbling registered on the other side of the door, he swallowed the thick paste in his throat and wiped sweaty palms down the front of his jeans. Christ. He'd probably drop at her feet if she opened the damn door.

The door finally did open, though, revealing Cassie in all her glory. Being nine o'clock at night, she had on her pajamas. Pink pajamas, no less. She looked different. She'd cut her long hair and lost weight. Cassie had always had a healthy figure. She looked this side of too thin now, her cheekbones more pronounced. Her big brown eyes had a haunted look in their depths.

Of course, he *hoped* she'd cooled off by now, that maybe she'd come around.

She folded her arms, shifted her weight onto her left foot, and cocked a brow. "What do you want, Ty?"

What did he want? To take her in his arms. Hold her. Spend half the night rediscovering all the ways her body fit against his. To hear her breathing beside him while he slept. Not that he did sleep. Or that he should risk trying to with her, given how he spent most of his nights. But he wanted the luxury of her beside him in bed all the same.

He knew going to the auction she likely wouldn't even *want* to see him, but he needed to try. So, he stepped over the threshold, moving into her personal space. Close enough her soft perfume floated around him. Chanel something or other. He couldn't recall the name, but, God, he loved the soft scent of it. She dabbed it behind her ears and between her breasts, and the scent made him yearn to search her skin for it.

"I needed to see you. You have no idea how much I missed you." Drumming up courage from God knew where, he smiled. "You owe me a date."

Yeah, and he owed Dean like twenty years' salary. Dean had loaned him the money to bid on Cassie at the auction. It would take him years to pay Dean back, but it would be worth it if he could get her to spend some time with him.

"I'm sorry you came all the way out here, Ty, but I can't go on a date with you." Cassie straightened her shoulders, which did nothing but press her breasts into his chest, and hiked her chin to a stubborn angle. "I've moved on."

Her words had the same impact now as they had hours ago. They hit his gut as surely as if she'd struck him. So she intended to play it like that.

He shook his head. "You're a damn stubborn woman, you know that? We argued. So loudly the neighbors pounded on the connecting wall. At some point, I told you to go to hell, and you stormed from my apartment and slammed the door so hard the walls shook. But that's all it was. An argument."

His mind filled with the memory of that long-ago night. He'd proposed to her, heart in his hands. She hadn't reacted the way he'd anticipated. After all the nights they'd spent wrapped around each other, she had the nerve to tell him she had no feelings for him beyond the physical. He'd called bullshit, hoping beyond hope he was right, that she cared more than she wanted him to believe, but all it had done was piss her off.

Now, her breathing ramped up several notches, her chest and shoulders heaving like she'd run a marathon. She stared, mouth open, then turned and stormed off. Seconds later, her bedroom door slammed.

"Why is he doing this?"

Her voice drifted down the hallway and Tyler rolled his eyes. She'd called for backup. Gray no doubt, who probably wanted to kick his ass. Tonight hadn't gone how he'd imagined it. His mother had made a point to tell him Cassie had grieved hard over his death. They'd been watching a movie with Dean and the girls when the commercial came, flashing Cassie's gorgeous face. Since coming home, he hadn't called or gone to see her because he found normal life hard to adjust to. Everything was too damn bright and too noisy, and he was overwhelmed.

One look at her smiling face, though, had the need to see her burning in his gut. After three years of trying not to forget, to remember every little nuance of her, his heart had taken the knowledge and run with it.

Now he almost regretted going to the auction, because if he didn't know better, he'd swear she was sorry he *wasn't* dead.

"It's been three years. I'm finally starting to move on. Why would he do this now?" Cassie's voice drifted down the hallway again. She paused, as if listening. Thirty seconds or so later, she came marching back to the front door. She looked down at her phone and touched a button on the screen. "You're on speaker, Marilyn."

"Ty, honey, I told you that auction wasn't a good idea."

At the sound of his mother's voice, he could only shake his head. "My mother? Out of all the people you could have called, you call my mother?" It gave him hope. That he was right, and she cared more than she wanted to let on. He took Cassie's phone from her hand and glanced down at it. His mother didn't need to be privy to this conversation. "I'll call you later, Ma. I love you."

Also something he'd regretted a lot over the last three years. Not telling her how much he appreciated her. Dean had been the golden boy, top of his class, always did what he was told and did it well. He was currently married and the vice president of the communications corporation he worked for.

Tyler had always been the rebellious kid who'd run with the wrong crowd and did everything anybody in a position of authority told him not to. He'd spent a lot of time over the last three years wondering if his mother knew how much he appreciated everything she'd sacrificed for them.

"I love you, too, sweetheart. Be gentle with her."

He disconnected the call and held Cassie's phone out to her, but she didn't take it. She stood staring, eyes wide, gaze searching his. One by one tears began to fall, and she pivoted, moving farther into the house. She stopped at the edge of the living room but didn't say anything. So, he closed the front door and followed, stopping several feet behind her.

He had to hand it to her. She wasn't coming apart at the seams. She simply stood, back stiff and straight, arms folded, staring out the floor-to-ceiling windows that made up her living room wall. He knew from previous experience those windows gave an unprecedented view of downtown Seattle and Elliott Bay beyond. They'd stood on her enormous deck more than once, her wrapped in his arms, looking out over the city, talking about dreams and futures.

"It's been three years." She spoke so softly he barely heard her, as if she were talking to herself, but not once did her voice waver. "Three years, Ty. Now suddenly here you are, alive and whole."

"I've always been whole, though why they let me live is beyond me."

He'd had three years to ponder this moment. Too much damn time to dream up everything he'd say to her. The problem was, he couldn't get the words to leave past the lump in his throat. He hadn't anticipated how powerful being in her presence again would be. He ached to wrap his arms around her and hold her until she stopped shaking, but he had no idea if she'd let him. Had no idea, either, if he could stand to be touched. He'd spent three years in what had essentially been solitary confinement. Alone with stone walls.

Since coming home, everything brought up memories he didn't want to remember anymore. Post-traumatic stress the doctor had said. Something as simple as his mother's hug could send him into a spiral to hell. None of which Cassie needed to see now.

So, he shoved his hands in his pockets.

"What happened to you? You went missing and then they couldn't find you. After a year went by, they stopped looking, assumed you were dead. We had a funeral."

"They ambushed us. Six of us were captured. I'm the only one who made it out. I think they were hoping to trade us for a few of their own." He swallowed hard, forcing back the memories. Now wasn't the time to relive the horror of those final days. She didn't need to know the gory details, either, or watch him unravel as the memories sucked him into the past. "They kept moving us, shuffling us around, trying to stay one step ahead of the units looking for us. I honestly had no idea how much time had passed or even what was happening. It was just a series of endless days and nights."

She finally turned to face him. "Why aren't you angry with me? I said some cruel things to you the last time we saw each other. You shouldn't even *want* to see me."

He looked down at the floor for a moment. He'd thought about this a lot, too.

"For a long time, I was. You didn't just turn down my proposal. You shoved it back in my face and made sure I knew how unimportant I was to you." He looked up then, pinning her with a direct stare. He had no intention of letting her slip past him this time. They were *going* to settle this once and for all, whatever that meant. He needed the closure. "Which was why I called bullshit. You run from anything even resembling commitment. You don't think I see you, but I do."

Or at least he had. Now they were strangers again, and everything inside of him rebelled against the idea. The thought alone brought up a deep well of anger he didn't know what to do with. They'd stolen three years of his life.

She wrapped her arms over her stomach, her voice small and dejected. "It doesn't change things."

He ducked down to look in her eyes. "Doesn't it?"

She met his gaze with a stubborn lift of her chin but hurt filled her eyes. "No, because…You're going back, aren't you?"

Phrased as a question, but her piercing gaze dared him to deny it, telling him she already knew the answer.

"I don't know. I've got psych evals first." And he knew

damn well what they'd find. He needed something to make him feel useful, not quite so fucked up, but they'd never put him back on active duty. He'd be lucky to get a desk job. "You, however, could at least have the balls to be honest with me."

He knew she had them. Cassie could be fierce when she wanted to be. She'd never let him hide. He wouldn't let her, either.

She stared at him, for what had to be the hundredth time since he arrived. When she didn't answer, he dared a step forward and closed the gap between them, hovering over her. So close the heat of her body infused his and her sweet, sweet perfume called to him like the lure of a siren's song. He ached to touch her, if only to remember the suppleness of her skin. To get lost in her in a blind attempt to chase away the hell living in his head.

"I remember. I remember the way you used to look at me, the way we held each other at night. Have the balls to be honest with me and tell me why you *really* turned me down." He had a feeling he knew, but he needed to hear her say the words.

Cassie lifted her chin to a defiant angle. "I'm not doing this with you again, Ty."

He wanted to laugh. God, he loved her feistiness. She'd been a challenge from the beginning, from the first corny line he'd tossed at her.

He'd been on leave the weekend he'd run into her. Her older brother, Nick, had been one of his best friends. He'd gone to the fireworks display at the Space Needle that night with Dean and some friends to honor Nick's memory and the memory of others they'd lost in the war. He'd met Cassie for the first time when she barreled into him. There she was, tipsy, wearing a skirt that showed more thigh than it covered and sexy, strappy little sandals that made her legs look a mile long. Who the hell wore heels to a Fourth of July celebration he didn't know, but she'd plowed into him so hard, she'd ended up in his arms. The awful pickup line he'd tossed at her had been an instinctive reaction. *"Aw, look who fell from heaven."*

She'd glared at him, but she hadn't been able to hide her smile, and he'd tossed several more at her to see that smile bloom. In the conversation that followed, he learned she was Nick's little sister, and she'd gone downtown for the same reason he had.

He pulled himself from the memories and refocused on her face.

"I need to hear you say the words." Like he needed air to breathe. He needed to know their relationship wasn't a figment of his vivid imagination. Needed it to ground him in the here and now, because he'd left a huge chunk of himself back in the fucking desert. "You owe me that much."

She fisted her hands at her sides and glared at him.

"Fine. Because your job scares the hell out of me. I couldn't do it, Ty. I lost Nick to that damn war. He went over there and didn't come back. I couldn't sit around waiting for you to die, too. I have friends and way too many customers whose husbands and brothers and sons have died over there. I started a new jewelry line. Did you know that? In honor of the fallen. The thought of losing you like that?" Her breathing hitched and her lower lip wobbled. A single tear made its way down her cheek, but she didn't acknowledge it. "But it happened anyway."

He'd met Nick when they'd stationed him at Joint Base Lewis–McChord after Basic. Nick had already been three years in. He was the kind of guy you couldn't help but like, who made friends with everybody. Five years ago, he deployed to Iraq, only to die months later when his Humvee rolled over an IED. Being the driver, he'd taken the brunt of the blast.

He had to hand it to Cassie. At least she was honest with him. He could work with that.

"I miss Nick every damn day, but I'm still here." He opened his arms, holding them out from his sides. To prove a point. Because despite knowing he'd likely jump out of his skin the first time she touched him, he still hoped she'd end up in his arms. He needed her there, needed her soft touch to chase away the demons.

He didn't know what to expect from her at this point, but an aching second passed in tense silence. She stared at him, visibly trembling, a few tears meandering their way down her cheeks. When he was sure she wouldn't say anything else, that he was getting nowhere with her, Cassie drew a sharp breath. She took that step, slid her hands up his chest. Her arms closed around his neck, and her body became a second skin.

Tyler sucked in a desperate breath and gritted his teeth. For a moment, he could only stand there and remember to drag in oxygen. Memories snapped into his mind faster than he could stop them. Unending days of sitting, alone, curled up in the corner of a dank cell. Too many damn nights terrified to sleep for fear he wouldn't wake up the next day.

That he'd never get to see *her* again.

His throat closed, taking his air supply with it, and he squeezed his eyes shut, willing himself to stay in the present. It wasn't real, but he could still feel that bastard's hot breath on his face.

"Ty?"

Her soft, familiar voice floated into his consciousness. The warmth of her hand settled on his chest, and he jumped, his eyes snapping open. Cassie stared at him, concern etched into the lines of her forehead. "What's the matter?"

He forced a smile, positive it trembled like the rest of him.

"I'm fine." One by one, he forced his limbs to relax. Jesus. He needed to calm the hell down. It was just Cassie.

"No, you're not. What's wrong?"

He shook his head. He wouldn't go into this with her. Not now. Maybe not ever. What he needed was her, in his arms, as close as he could get her. Maybe then the goddamn demons would stop chasing him down.

Maybe then he'd finally stop shaking.

He reached out slowly, half afraid she'd disappear the moment he touched her, and cupped her cheek. When his palm slid over the warm suppleness of her skin, when she didn't, in fact, evaporate into the ether, he allowed himself to draw a breath. God, she was real. It was a stupid thing to think, but it awed him all the same.

Encouraged, he slid his arms loosely around her, tugging her against him. The instant her soft body hit his, her lush, full breasts pushing into his chest, his whole body lit up. Like someone had set his blood on fire. He wanted to laugh. He hadn't thought about sex or anything like it in three damn years, had been sure once that his dick had shriveled up from lack of use. One touch from her, though, and his cock pulsed behind his zipper. A groan escaped him, every inch of him relaxing into the sweetness of her. God, she was heaven, and he wanted to get lost in her.

Unable to help himself, he bent to brush his mouth over hers. Once. Twice. She had the most incredible mouth. So full and supple. When she lifted onto her toes, the last shred of his resistance went up in a puff of smoke. Three years of longing, of not knowing if he'd see her again, caved in on him. He cupped her face in his palms and drank her in, spent long minutes refamiliarizing himself with the shape of her lips.

She moaned, a soft little purr at the back of her throat that had always driven him crazy, and her hands burrowed beneath the back of his shirt.

He groaned again. Christ, he couldn't help himself. If this was a dream, he prayed he'd never wake up. She'd told him once she adored the heat of his skin. Whenever possible, her hands had always been up his shirt. He'd gotten into the habit of not tucking them in when not in uniform.

She didn't disappoint now. Her hands stroked upward, taking his shirt with it, and he pulled back to whip it off over his head. The shirt hit the floor with a soft *shush* of fabric, and Cassie took his hand, leading him to the couch. Once there, she released him and nodded. "Sit."

In her quiet demand, the answer to his problem presented itself. If sex was where she was comfortable, that's where he'd start—in the bedroom. Hell, they'd started that way originally. On that Fourth of July night, she'd ended up in his bed. They'd spent the night making love and talking.

Now it meant he'd have to touch her. He'd have to risk drawing up those ugly memories, but he *hoped* she'd let down a wall or two. So, he took the idea and ran with it.

He dropped onto the sofa behind him and crooked a finger at her. She shook her head, sinking to her knees at his feet instead and reached for the button on his jeans. As she popped it free and slid down the zipper, her slender fingers brushed his cock, hardening him to the point of pain.

He sucked in a hissing breath and shackled her wrist. "Uh-uh. I need you closer."

It had been too damn long. If she put her mouth on him now, he'd go off like a goddamn Roman candle. He needed to take this slowly, or he'd embarrass himself.

For once in her life, Cassie didn't argue but allowed him to pull her off the floor and slide onto his lap, straddling his thighs. When she leaned into him, pushing her gorgeous tits into his chest, he feared he'd bust the seam on his jeans. How the hell had he ever lived without that feeling? How had he ever thought he could let her go?

He kissed her softly, luxuriating in her mouth on his, and reached up her tank to close his hands around her breasts. She wasn't wearing a bra, and her breasts were deliciously free. God, she had the most fantastic tits. Full and round. She wasn't getting a damn thing out of him playing with them like this, but Christ. It had been three years since he'd had his hands on her. He couldn't resist massaging them or running his thumbs back and forth across her distended nipples. He might have whipped her shirt off and replaced his hands with his mouth, except she reached between them and closed her hand around his cock. She stroked him slowly, from base to tip, sending pleasure curling through him.

"Holy mother of God." He closed his eyes, sucking in a desperate breath between clenched teeth, and abandoned her breasts to shackle her wrist. "Easy, baby. You keep doing that and I'm going to embarrass myself in about two seconds."

For three years, nobody had touched him with anything resembling kindness. Cassie had a soft touch, the supple skin of her hands as close to heaven as he'd ever gotten, second only to the warm tightness of being buried deep inside her.

Cassie, however, was stubborn and willful and so fucking beautiful. She kept stroking, so slowly he couldn't be sure if he wanted her to speed up or stop. She knew how drive him out of his mind, how he liked to be touched, the right pressure, the perfect speed…

His thighs tensed, his feet bracing on the floor, and he dropped his head back against the couch cushions. "Baby, I'm serious. It's been a while for me."

As if her hand wasn't enough, she scooted forward, nestling the length of his cock between her thighs. So damned close the moist heat of her radiated to him. She leaned forward to rub her nipples against his chest. God, her breasts had always been his biggest fantasy.

"I don't care. Let it go, Ty." She brushed her mouth across his, the softest, sweetest of kisses. "We need this. *I* need this."

The quiet vulnerability in her voice made him open his eyes. She stared at him again, eyes at half-mast but still searching. In that one tiny moment, something shifted between them. He'd long since recognized the silent exchange. An acknowledgment of need.

He relaxed back into the sofa cushions and let her have her way with him. Let her take his world, all the goddamn nightmares, the horror of the last three years, the images he couldn't forget no matter how much he tried, and spin it out of control.

Both hands wrapped around his shaft, she stroked from base to tip, so slowly his toes curled. When he sucked in a hissing breath, she flicked her tongue over his lips. Damn her. She had him on his knees, and she knew it.

"Payback, baby. Payback." Jesus. Shaking and breathless, his muscles tightened to the point of pain, his body poised on the desperate edge of release. Somehow, he'd imagined this moment differently. He'd wanted to take her with him, but he couldn't move if he tried. He could barely breathe.

She leaned forward again, rubbing her nipples against his chest, and his balls drew tight against his body. "Look at me."

Her demand was quiet but no less powerful, and he did as she bade. Heat filled her eyes, hunger illuminating her from within. "You are so damned beautiful, you know that?"

It was pathetic how short the bliss lasted. Her supple fingers moved up and down his cock like she had all the time in the world to torment him. Yet each stroke hauled him closer to the edge. Another soft, slow stroke and his orgasm rushed over him out of nowhere.

"Cassie..." His garbled warning came seconds before every muscle tensed in a sudden rush. Like a wildfire burning through a dry field, the bliss swallowed him whole, leaving him quivering and gasping and completely at her mercy. He didn't know if he even remembered to breathe.

Cassie stroked him through every incredible pulse, her grip loosening, her fingers grazing his now super sensitive skin, which did nothing but extend the pleasure. Leaving him a gasping, trembling heap.

When the last erotic pulse faded, he collapsed back against the couch, panting and spent. He reached out blindly, found her thigh, and stroked his hand upward. "Have I mentioned I missed you?"

She flat-out fucking amazed him. He'd expected being this close to her would set off another flashback, that he wouldn't be able to tolerate her touch. But his need for her had been so great, so overwhelming, he'd lost sight of everything but her. And he hadn't a fucking clue how to tell her what that meant to him.

Cassie didn't respond. Instead, she went silent. So still he pried his eyes open.

She sat staring at him, wide-eyed, chest heaving, soft, ragged breaths puffing against his mouth, looking as shell-shocked as he felt. "One night."

He shook his head. The sleepy lull of postorgasm fatigue already pulled at him, his brain lost in a fog. "One night what?"

"You said I owe you a date. I'll give you one night. This one. But that's it. This isn't real, Ty. We broke up, and I've moved on. This is just delayed grief or something. We've already proven we don't work."

Panic set his heart pounding his rib cage as what she meant settled over him. Jesus, he couldn't let her go now…

He shook his head, searching her eyes for some trace of the girl he'd known. For some small measure of proof he hadn't imagined she felt anything for him at all. "It was a fight, Cassie. Albeit a poorly timed one, but it was just a fight. We both said things we regretted that night."

She shook her head, those big brown eyes still wide, still vulnerable. "I can't do this with you again. I need to move on, and I need you to let me. I can't deny seeing you again brings it all back up, but this is just breakup sex, Ty. Nothing more."

She paused and looked down at his lap. Long, aching seconds ticked out. He could only watch her eyes. His chest and stomach were covered in the evidence that she had power over him, that only her touch could soothe the monster raging inside of him. He couldn't let her go now.

Her throat bobbed before she finally looked up at him again. "I'll give you one night, but no more. In the morning, you go home, and we don't see each other again."

He wanted to argue with her. She was telling him good-bye again, but he refused to listen. He had to believe somewhere inside she loved him the way he loved her. He had to. Or the horror of the last three years really would win.

Except he couldn't give her what she wanted, either.

When he'd come over tonight, he hadn't been sure what to expect from her. It depended on what side of her she intended to give him. The carefree party girl who insisted she didn't need anybody…or the vulnerable girl who plastered herself against his side, laid her head on his chest, and told him her hopes and dreams.

He had no idea, either, how she'd take what he had to tell her next. There was too much water under their bridge, too many things they needed to discuss. She was right. Sex was a complication, but damn it. It had been three long fucking years, and he needed to be as close to her as possible. Maybe if he could hold her awhile, he'd stop feeling as if he were coming apart at the seams.

"I don't agree on one night. That wasn't lip service, babe. I'm not giving up on you." He swallowed past the lump forming in his throat. Despite the tightness in his chest and the voice in his head telling him to shut the hell up, he dragged in a breath and forced himself to say the words. She deserved honesty. "But I can't stay all night."

Yeah. He'd essentially told her that when they finished feasting on each other, he'd be going home. He had to. No way could he spend the night with her. He had no intention of letting her see how he spent his nights. If he was lucky, he tossed and turned, *unable* to sleep. On those nights, he'd walk the floor of his bedroom or try watching TV to drown out the shit in his head.

It was the nights he *could* sleep that got him, when the exhaustion pulled him under. The dreams were more vivid on those nights. He usually woke drenched in sweat, heart hammering like a freight train. His mother had told him more than once that he cried out in his sleep. Sometimes sobbing like a goddamn child. Sometimes screaming for the team members he couldn't save.

Often, he'd wake to find his mother standing in the bedroom doorway, worry creasing her forehead. Sometimes, the dreams would morph, and he'd wake to find her perched on the edge of his bed, singing to him. A soft, soothing song she'd sung to him as a child. On those nights, the dreams morphed. He'd watch *her* die, over and over, in god-awful ways, and he'd wake in a panic.

No way in hell could he let Cassie see that. To see he'd come back half a man. Or to risk having those kinds of nightmares about her.

No. Maybe sometime in the future, when the dreams faded. They had to fade. At some point, the shit in his head had to go away. It couldn't last forever, could it? But the last thing he wanted was for her to have to watch it happen.

He'd hoped she'd ask why or that somehow she'd understand, but the light left her eyes, telling him he wasn't about to get any of that. Her smile fell, and in the next breath, a wall went up between them.

She slid off his lap and left the room. "Then maybe you should just leave now."

Chapter Three

Cassie shoved the bedroom door closed and crossed to the bed, where she climbed up and flopped down on her back, staring at the ceiling. Its textured pattern blurred behind a veil of tears. Christ, she'd done too much damn crying in the last week, but seeing Tyler tonight had shaken her foundation.

She'd allowed her relief at seeing him alive pull her back in. Had allowed herself to get caught up in *it*, that certain something that pulled them together like the ocean tides to the moon. If he hadn't stopped, she had no doubt she'd have spent the night with him. Happily. Deliriously.

Because she'd missed him.

Except he *had* stopped it, and the ache in her chest threatened to crush her. Of all things for him to tell her, that he wouldn't stay had been the nail in her coffin. It would already hurt to watch him leave, watch him walk out of her life again. If she was going to do it, then she wanted the *whole* night. If he couldn't—wouldn't—stay, then he could just go now.

The bedroom door opened with a rush of air, and she turned her head. Tyler strode into the room. Having cleaned up and donned his shirt again, he moved toward the bed with calm determination. Her heart hammered. She should've known he'd follow her. He'd never been one to give up easily. Whenever she pushed, he wasn't afraid to push back.

Except he hesitated at the foot of the bed, staring at her for long moments. Tyler was different. Something haunted and dark hovered in the recesses of his eyes. He'd always been a tender lover, but this time, he'd touched her with the same reverence he had when he kissed her after the auction. It brought up questions she didn't know if she wanted the answers to. What did they do to him that the confident, sexy soldier she'd met four years ago now hesitated to touch her?

His presence in her room, however, unnerved her. It meant deep down somewhere, he was still the same man she'd known. The man who'd shown up at her penthouse at nine o'clock at night because he had to see her. She couldn't hide from him. He always seemed to see right through her.

"What are you doing, Ty?" Palms already beginning to sweat, she sat upright in a vain attempt to put some distance between them.

"I have something to say to you before I leave." He didn't bother to wait for her response, but crawled up onto the bed. When he reached her, he pushed her knees apart and moved between them, forcing her to lie back before settling himself on his elbows.

Tyler wasn't a small man by any means. Six foot four to her five foot six, he towered over her. Though he'd gotten a lot thinner over the last three years, his weight alone still prevented her from rising. How many times had she been in this exact position? Tyler's favorite position had always been missionary, and she'd been happy to oblige because he always made sure when he went, he took her with him.

The intensity in his gaze now, however, captured her attention. He'd never been one to hide his emotions. When she pissed him off, he told her so. When he'd fallen in love with her, he'd told her that, too. While holding her so tight she might as well have been a part of him, he'd whispered the words in ear. *I'm in love with you, Cassie.*

Now something intense moved behind his eyes as he stroked her hair back from her face with the tip of his index finger, tracing her features. The shell of her ear. Across her jawline. Over her bottom lip. As if, perhaps, he were refamiliarizing himself. In seconds flat, he mesmerized her, left her too caught up in him to find the will to push him off.

"I know this is a lot for you to deal with right now. I suspect Mom is correct, that you've just had the wind knocked out of you, but you learn something when you face death day after day. I learned who was important to me, who the people were I'd have given my last breath to see one more time, and for the record, you're on the top of that list." He leaned his head beside her ear and nipped at the fleshy lobe. "I let you get away from me once. That's a mistake I don't intend to make twice."

The husky rumble of his voice in her ear had her panties dampening. His warm, ragged breath sent shivers down her spine. Sex with Ty was like everything else with him—

intense. When he made love to her, he stared at her like he could see right through her. Then held her afterward like he'd never let her go.

After losing Nick, she'd closed off her heart. His death had taken its toll on their family. They'd lost their mother to a cruel fate. Some dumbass texting on a cell phone had run a red light, the exact moment her mother's car had been in the middle of the intersection. She'd suffered a slow death, lingering for days before passing.

Nick's death had left a gaping hole in their family. Her father hadn't been the same since. He'd gone within himself and hadn't come back out yet. Cassie had walled off her heart, because it was easier not to care than to risk losing someone again.

And then came Ty. He'd broken down her defenses, made her want something more for the first time, and it had scared the hell out of her.

"That's not your decision," she said. Desperate not to let him know he'd gotten to her, desperate not to feel it, she shoved against his chest.

Tyler didn't appear to be listening. Instead, he skimmed his mouth along her jawline, nipping with his teeth. He let out an agonized groan and nipped at her bare shoulder, sending a shower of sparks shooting from the point of contact straight down between her thighs. A soft gasp left her mouth, and Tyler lifted his head, brow arched, eyes daring her to deny him.

"Maybe not, but you of all people ought to know I don't give up easily."

She rolled her eyes, going for indifferent, but her clit throbbed. She ached to feel his mouth everywhere. Oh, she remembered all right. Over the last three years, she'd masturbated to the vivid memory of his talented tongue buried between her thighs a lot.

"For now, I'll go." He rose off her and sat back on his knees. The playful heat left his eyes, his expression sobering. "For the record, there *is* a reason I'm not staying. I half hoped you'd ask and half hoped you wouldn't. Right now, I'm just not ready for that particular talk. It's heavy, and I don't want to go there. Eventually, I'm going to have to, but now? It's too raw."

He shook his head. A wisp of pain flitted through the recesses of his eyes, but he drew a breath and the look vanished. He climbed from the bed and bent over her, his right hand braced against the mattress.

"Mark my words, though. You won't be getting away from me so easily again."

He pressed a lingering kiss to her lips, so light and tender tears welled in her eyes; then he straightened and left the room. She followed the sounds of his progress down the hallway and through the living room. When the front door closed with a quiet snap, the tears finally broke loose, and she let them.

* * *

Bright and too damn early the next morning, the annoying buzz of her doorbell woke her from a dead sleep. She rolled over and covered her head with her pillow. Maybe if she pretended to be dead, they'd go away. She'd spent most of the night staring at the ceiling, trying not to call Tyler and invite him back. The clock had passed three before she'd finally fallen asleep.

Gray had called somewhere around nine, wanting to make sure she was okay. He'd called four times, actually, but she wasn't in the mood to call him back. What on earth could she tell him? That Tyler being alive had rocked her back on her heels? That his sudden place in her life again left her struggling with what she wanted?

When the incessant buzzing came again in rapid succession, she gave in and, with an annoyed huff, flung back the covers and sat up. No sooner had she grabbed her robe off the ottoman at the end of her bed than the damn sound came again.

"All right, all right. Geez, I'm coming." She grumbled in the general direction of the door as she made her way, eyes half closed, through the apartment. After undoing the locks, she yanked the door open, glaring at whoever the hell was on the other side.

Gray, as it turned out, leaned in her doorway, in a pair of jogging pants and a T-shirt. Cleary he'd stopped by while out for a morning jog, but he looked way too awake and put together for so early. It didn't help that he held a box from her favorite bakery and a large cup of Starbucks.

"Morning, sunshine."

She folded her arms. "Why are you on my doorstep this damn early in the morning?"

"You haven't returned my calls. You could have at least called to tell me you were okay." He wiggled the box his hands and grinned, ear to freaking ear. "Besides, I brought breakfast. From Le Panier. Thought perhaps if I came bearing gifts you'd let me keep my balls for waking you up. Maddie's rather fond of them."

The corners of her mouth twitched. Damn him. They'd been friends long enough that he knew exactly how to get to her. She wanted to be angry with him. She needed to be. He knew how hard it had been for her to get over thinking Tyler had died, how hard it had been to pick herself up and keep going.

Drawing up her last stubborn ounce of irritation, she poked his chest. "You'd deserve it if I did lop them off. How could you sabotage me that way and not even give me a hint? And don't tell me you had nothing to do with last night, because that has you written all over it. You did something similar to Maddie last year."

Four years ago, Gray and Maddie had been an item…until she discovered the editor she'd been working with *owned* the company. At the time, he'd worked at the publishing house under an assumed name, in an effort to prove the lies spreading about how he'd come to own the company wrong. He'd planned to tell his employees, but someone in the company leaked the story to the paper first. Maddie had discovered the truth before he had the chance to tell her.

After spending three years missing her, Gray had concocted a scheme to win her back. He had Christina set Maddie up on a blind date. He didn't tell her until they were due to meet at the bachelor auction that the man she'd been chatting with online had been Gray in disguise. Cassie had told him from the beginning the charade was a bad idea, but Gray had been desperate. In the end, it had almost cost him their relationship.

"Why the hell would you do something like again?" Cassie asked.

His smile fell, his expression sobering. "Honest. I didn't know. He did that all on his own. I would never do that to you."

The truth was, the gesture would almost have melted her defenses. She had the heart of a romantic. She preferred skirts over pants, pink over black, and had a love affair with gorgeous heels. She'd even designed a line of jewelry, delicate pieces with a feminine flair. The Romance Collection.

Gray was right, though. The gesture screamed of Tyler. It would be just like him to show up with a grin and go, "Surprise!"

"Besides." Gray shook his head, lines forming around his mouth. "You missed him. You can deny it, but I was there when you got the call, and I've been there every day since. His death hit you hard. You needed last night as much as he did."

She sighed, relenting, and took the coffee from his hand, sipping at the much needed dose of caffeine. He knew how she liked her coffee, too: a vanilla latte with extra foam.

Once bolstered, she stepped back and pulled the door open wider. "Fine. You got me there." She nodded at the box in his hands, unable to hide her smile. "What'd you bring me?"

"An assortment of croissants." Gray grinned and jiggled the box, his voice singsong. "There's a *roulé aux noix* in here."

Cassie's mouth watered. Oh, now he had her. Le Panier was her favorite place, hands down. An authentic French bakery-slash-bistro in Pike Place Market, they served everything from sandwiches to delectable pastries. The *roulé aux noix* was her favorite—buttery, flaky goodness filled with a mixture of sugar and walnuts.

"God, I love you for knowing me so well. For that alone, you get to come in." Stomach now grumbling, she snatched the box from his hands. "And I'll let you keep your balls. Wouldn't want to disappoint Maddie. She and I are just becoming friends."

Gray chuckled as he closed the door, his quiet footsteps behind her as she made her way into the kitchen. "I didn't come find you last night because I figured you needed your space."

She let out a huff of a laugh as she set her coffee onto the counter and turned, pulling a small plate from a cupboard. "No you didn't. You were afraid I'd lop 'em off right there."

He slid onto a stool at the breakfast bar, folding his hands on the counter. "No, I'm serious. I left you several messages. When you didn't call me back, I was tempted to come find you, make sure you were okay, but Maddie forced me to leave you be."

The soft tone of his voice stopped her. She set the plate on the counter and turned sideways to look at him. "I appreciate the concern. Tell her I said thank you. I needed time to think. I got your messages. I had plans to call you this morning, but you beat me to it."

He quirked a brow. "I take it he found you?"

She nodded. Turning back to the box, she opened the lid and bent to inhale the luscious aroma. After snatching out the *roulé aux noix*, she set it on the plate and joined him at the breakfast bar. She took a moment to bite into the sweet, buttery goodness, moaning around her mouthful. "You're a god, Gray. An absolute god."

"You're welcome." He nudged her with an elbow. "So? Don't go quiet on me now. What happened? Tyler never came back. You disappeared. I figured the two of you were together, but clearly he's not here."

She wiped her mouth with a napkin and shrugged. Remorse rose over her, and she slid off her stool to fetch her coffee from the counter.

"He found me in the parking lot and kissed me. I assumed he was playing a cruel joke, because he ought to be pissed at me. *I* wouldn't want to see me again. I spent three years telling myself I needed to get over him but silently praying he'd show up one day. I may not have wanted to marry the man, but dead is something altogether different, you know? I was just so damn glad he was alive. And suddenly there he was." She peered at him as she tipped the warm liquid into her mouth. "What do you think I did?"

Gray nodded, his mouth forming a thin, disapproving line. "You insulted him."

"And left him eating my dust." She moved around the

island and reclaimed her seat beside him with a sigh. "He came over later."

"I'm assuming he didn't stay."

She took another bite of the pastry, allowing herself a moment to enjoy the much needed sugar before answering him.

"I asked him to leave." She peered down at her plate, that ugly mix of remorse and need caught in her chest again. "I wanted him to stay and he couldn't, and I just couldn't do it. For three years, I've been running from the way I feel about him. From what I really wanted, deep down. On your wedding day, I got honest with myself. What you and Maddie have? I want that. I don't know what to do with it, but I can't deny anymore that I want it."

He wrapped a beefy arm around her shoulders, hugging her against the warmth of his side. "So go get it."

She shook her head as she straightened away from him. "He has psych evals first, but I think he wants to go back. Maybe it's crazy and mixed up, but I can't watch him do it. I just can't. Especially now."

Gray sat silent for a moment. "I'm guessing he wants to go back because it's easier."

The somber tone of his voice had her looking over at him. "Than what?"

"Being home. The best thing Arthur ever did for me was take me home that night, but it wasn't an easy process. I got so used to living with my father's anger, with surviving from day to day, that living with Arthur, being taken care of, not having to fight, didn't feel safe. I kept expecting the bottom to drop out from under me. I can't imagine what Tyler went through over there, but I've heard it isn't easy coming home."

He finally glanced over at her, and the haunted look in his eyes told her he remembered his birth father. Arthur Bradbury, owner of the midsized publishing company Gray had since taken over, had adopted Gray at the age of fourteen. He was a kindhearted old man. One who'd cared enough to yank a small boy from the dangerous home he'd grown up in. Scars covered Gray's back, the leftovers of beatings his birth father had given him. Experiences he shouldn't have had to endure.

Gray slid off his stool, peering down at her, and she tipped her head back to look into his face. "Don't do what I did. I let Maddie go when I should have fought for her, and it cost us three years we can't get back. I was afraid if she saw how damaged I was, she wouldn't want me."

She reached out to take his hand, squeezing his fingers. "Your scars wouldn't have bothered her."

"Mmm. I know that now. You told me once you regretted hurting Tyler, the day he asked you to marry him, you remember?"

"I remember." She didn't have to ask to know where he intended to go with this line of questioning. He'd tell her the same thing she told Maddie seven months ago.

When Maddie had ended her relationship with Gray a second time, Cassie had gone over to smooth things out and gave her some advice straight from the heart. *"I had a Gray once. Tyler was everything to me, and I lost him. Trust me. You'll regret not having Gray more than you'll ever regret loving him."*

Hadn't she had the same thought last night, that if she could do it over, she'd do it differently?

Gray nudged her shoulder, pulling her from the memory. "This is your chance. By some miracle, he's come back. Don't let this opportunity pass you by."

He waited, as if expecting an answer, but she couldn't give him one. She didn't know how.

"I have to go. Maddie and I are going out for breakfast." He dropped his arm and stood for a moment, staring at her. "Promise you'll call me if you need me?"

She smiled. "I will."

"Good." He kissed the top of her head and headed for the door, pausing as he pulled it open. "Think about what I said, okay?"

He didn't give her time to respond, closing the door with a quiet snap.

Cassie stared down at the "sugar bomb," as Gray so often called them, her heart heavy. He was right, of course. She'd spent the last three years wishing she could take back everything she'd told Tyler the day he'd asked her to marry him.

Only the regret had come because she'd thought him dead. That was normal, right? To wish you had one more chance with your loved one, to say the things you should have told them while they lived?

Except Tyler was alive, and she was reeling from it all. She'd been trying to forget him, desperate to move on with her life, and in one night, a single moment in time, he'd done what he had when she met him—turned her life on its head.

Chapter Four

T y."

At the sound of Cassie's surprised voice, Tyler stopped pacing and turned. She stood frozen on the other side of the threshold, still in the pink pajamas she'd had on last night, wide-eyed and stunned.

"What are you doing here so early?" She folded her arms, looking at him like he'd lost his mind.

Hell, he probably had. He'd come over only last night, and it was barely 9:00 a.m., but he had to see her. Last night, he'd dreamt about *her*. They'd tortured her, and he'd had to watch her die. He'd woken in a panic. As soon as the sky beyond his window began to lighten, breaking up the shadows pervading his room, he'd borrowed his mother's car and come straight here. Traffic from Renton wasn't bad, but it was the longest drive of his life. There were a surprising number of people on the road, most of them likely heading to church.

He needed to prove to himself she really was okay, to see her with his own two eyes. Despite knowing he'd likely woken her up, waiting the few minutes it took for her to answer the door had only amped up his stress. His mind had filled with ugly images. His heart hammered in his throat. He was sweating for crying out loud.

The sight of her, though, eased the panic seated in his chest. Even if she closed the door in his face, he wouldn't be sorry he'd come. For that singular moment, looking into her big, beautiful eyes and seeing her unharmed calmed the shaking he'd woken with.

When he didn't say anything, Cassie quirked a brow.

He shook his head, at a loss to explain. "I had to see you."

Yeah. Good move, Benson. He'd told her pretty much the same thing yesterday.

Not waiting for her response, Tyler stepped across the threshold. He stood for a moment, hovering over her, afraid that if he touched her those awful images would come again. He lifted his trembling hands anyway to cup her cheeks. When she didn't, in fact, evaporate, he blew out a relieved breath.

"Jesus. You're real." He released her and took a step back.

Concern took shape in her eyes as her gaze scanned down his body. "Ty, I can see you shaking. Are you okay?"

"Yeah." An irrational, half-cocked laugh escaped him. God, he probably sounded like a freakin' lunatic. He rubbed the back of his neck. "Yeah, I am now."

Cassie took a step toward him. "Are you sure?"

"Yeah. Yeah, I'm okay. Bad dream." He waved a flippant

hand in the air, praying she'd let it go, and pivoted, pacing several steps out into the vestibule.

God, he was making an ass out of himself. Here he was, on her doorstep at nine in the morning, shaking like a leaf in a windstorm. She'd have questions, no doubt. Ones he had no desire to answer.

To cover himself and stave off those questions, he turned back toward her and folded his arms. "You still owe me a date."

For a long moment she didn't say anything. Her eyes worked his face, reaching and searching in a way that made him feel naked, like he'd bared his demons. Finally, she arched a brow. "You came all the way over here at nine in the morning to remind me of that?"

He shook his head. Christ. He really was screwing this up. "I just needed to see you."

Watching her, the same idea he'd had yesterday flitted through his mind again, and he allowed himself to run with it. He'd decided something on the way over. She was bound and determined to keep him at arm's length, but he had every intention of breaking down her defenses. To find out once and for all whether or not he was right—that she really did care more than she let on.

If he was lucky, he'd cover having made an ass of himself, and she'd soften enough to agree to go out with him.

"I also believe I owe you, and I decided I didn't want to wait." He closed the door, then sank to his knees at her feet and sat for a moment, peering up at her. Waiting. They'd done this enough times he wouldn't have to tell her what he wanted. This had been her idea once upon a time. In a playful moment, she'd giggled and pointed at the floor. *On your knees, slave.*

Now those gorgeous brown eyes lowered to half-mast. Steeling himself for the contact, he skimmed his palms up her thighs and over her hips. Like last night, the panic never came. The last, leftover wisps of this morning's ugly dreams evaporated, lost in the feel of her body beneath his hands.

When he reached the waistband of her pajama pants, he stopped and waited, peering up at her. She had to feel him shaking, but he focused on her eyes. Every inch of him waited for her to stop him, to tell him no and demand him to leave.

She didn't. Her shoulders slumped, her perfectly polished nails grazing his scalp as she slid her fingers into his hair. "This makes three times you've ambushed me, Ty."

"I happen to like surprising you. Keeps you on your toes." He smiled as he tugged her pants down, taking her underwear with them, helping her step out of them. Then he caressed her thighs again, allowing himself a moment to enjoy the suppleness of her skin. Smooth, like creamy butter, and so damn soft. God, he'd missed this, the simplicity of being able to touch her.

When he stroked his thumbs over her outer lips, opening her, her breathing hitched. The delicate skin of her inner folds glistened in the low overhead lights. Unable to resist tasting her, he dipped his tongue in, a tender stroke along her slit, and a shudder moved through her that he felt in every cell. So he moved in again, this time flicking her clit. She let out a low, agonized moan. Her body relaxed, her hips bowing into him.

"That's my girl." He ached to dive in, to grip her tight little ass in his hands and bury his face in her scent, in her heat. For so many months he'd thought he'd never see her again. To get to touch her was like getting his hands on a piece of heaven. He wanted to lose himself and every godforsaken memory in her.

Until there wasn't anything left *but* her. He needed to feel her come apart in his hands. For her fingers to fist in his hair and pull him in. And he needed, more than he needed to draw his next breath, to feel her shuddering in his arms.

He wanted this to be good for *her*, too. Her orgasms were always better when he went slowly, when he indulged his senses. Those were the ones that caught her by surprise, that left her breathless and shaking.

So, he forced himself to take his time, nuzzled her instead, nudging her mound with his nose, enjoying the musky, sweet scent of her. Stroked her sensitive inner thighs, letting his thumbs graze her lips and licking softly at her.

Cassie, however, was Cassie: a beautiful, demanding, and stubborn woman used to getting what she wanted. She gripped his head in her hands, already pulling at him. "Goddamn it, Ty, stop teasing."

He chuckled but didn't move any faster. For far too many months, he'd thought he'd never get to experience this again.

"Sorry, baby, but I aim to take my time." He bent his head, sucking her clit into his mouth, and let it pop free.

Her quiet moan made his cock ache. She was heaven, the sweetest fruit.

"God, I missed this. Being able to touch you, to feel your reactions. You taste incredible. Hot and musky and sweet." He was rambling. Experience had taught him that talking to her, telling her how he wanted her, made her hot.

She didn't disappoint, letting out another moan, her knees beginning to shake.

To help support her, he guided her backward, until she came up against the wall, and leaned in. He stroked her with the flat of his tongue, a long, slow swipe that ended with a flick against the underside of her clit. "I'm going to enjoy the hell out of feeling you come around my tongue."

She moaned again, a sound of desperation. "Oh, God. Please."

"Please what?" He needed to hear her say the words.

She gripped the sides of his head hard, pulling him deeper into her. "I need this."

"So do I." He sucked on her clit again, only enough to drive her insane, to rush her to the edge, and released her. "Say it, Cassie. Tell me what you want."

Panting and breathless, she finally gave in, letting her hands drop to her sides. "Make me come, Ty. God, send me to the moon."

"You got it, baby." He didn't hold back this time, didn't tease, but gripped her ass in his hands and buried his face in her heat, licking and sucking at her swollen clit with abandon. When he inserted a finger, stroking her inner walls, her body went rigid. She gasped and held her breath, her whole body shaking, her hips bucking, riding his mouth like she owned him.

God, he loved it. She did own him, and he wasn't even sure she knew it or believed it, but he aimed to prove it to her. He held her tight in his hands, supporting her as he stroked and licked and sucked through every pulse, determined to extend her pleasure as long as possible.

Finally, she drew in a long, sharp breath, the sound of someone who'd been underwater for too long, and went limp. Breathless and panting, her knees were shaking so much he wondered what, if anything, held her up.

Tyler pushed to his feet and scooped her off the floor, then turned and headed for her bedroom. There, he laid her on the bed, crawled up beside her, and tucked her against his side.

She rested her head in the crook of his shoulder but her body remained stiff beneath his fingers. "One night, Ty. That's all I can give you. We can't keep doing this. I need to move on."

"Then we're stuck, babe, because I can't stay. Not yet. And I'm not willing to let you go. I refuse to believe you don't care."

"It doesn't change things. You're still going back, and I can't watch you do it."

He sighed. At some point, he'd have to be honest with her. By holding back, he only delayed the inevitable.

"You're right. I do want to go back. I want to catch those bastards. They mentioned taking me on as a correspondent, pending psych evals, but if they'll let me, yeah, I want to go.

If I can help in some capacity to take those fuckers down, make them pay for what they did?"

He closed his eyes and bit back the anger swelling in his chest. She didn't need to hear this crap, to have deal with his problems. At the same time, he couldn't stop the memories from rising, and for a moment, he couldn't say anything. The too familiar shaking started in his hands, spreading outward, and the memories sucked him in. Only the soft scent of her perfume kept him grounded in the here and now. He banded his arms around her, holding on to the shred of sanity he still had.

She was quiet for so long he tensed, waiting for the denial some part of him knew was coming. Finally, she drew a heavy breath and sat up, pulling away from him. She scooted to the edge of the bed and sat there for a moment.

"I'm sorry for what you went through, I really am, but I can't watch you do it again. I can't. You should just go." For the second time in as many days, she got up and walked away from him, striding into the attached bathroom.

At least this time she didn't slam the door. It closed behind her with a quiet snap, but the sound resounded through the room.

Determined not to give up, he crossed his arms and stayed where he was. She had to come back out sometime, so he'd wait. Took her five minutes, but eventually the door opened.

She darted a glance at him as she crossed to her dresser—painted white and topped by a three-tiered jewelry box and no less than a half dozen perfume bottles—and opened the top drawer. "Care to tell me why you're really here so early?"

"Couldn't sleep." It was a vague answer, and on some level, he knew he owed her the truth, but he had no desire to watch her face when he said the words. He hadn't slept more than a couple hours each night since he'd gotten home. Too much quiet. Too much time to think. Reminded him too damn much of the cell in Iraq. When he did manage to sleep, the dreams were never-ending.

Somewhere deep down, he knew he could never really be with her until he opened up to her about what he'd been through, until he told her the real reason he couldn't stay. But he had no desire to tell her.

She didn't look at him as she pulled a pair of light blue panties from the drawer and stepped into them. "A week passed after that morning your mother called me with the news, and then you showed up at the auction. What were you hoping to accomplish with that stunt?"

"I didn't call you because I didn't think you wanted to see me." Okay, so that was honest. He'd spent too much time re-hashing their last argument, until he'd convinced himself if he did show up on her penthouse, she'd slam the door in his face. "But I saw the commercial. They flashed your picture as one of the bachelorettes, and I couldn't stay away. I wasn't hoping for anything, except to see you in person."

Dean had been the one to finally convince him. They'd been sitting on the couch, watching whatever movie had been on TV that night. His brother had taken one look at him and pulled his wallet from his back pocket, handing him a credit card. *"Go get her. Go see your girl. At the very least, you'll get the closure you need."*

Ty had stared at the TV for long after the commercial had changed, the dejection weighing on him, pulling him down. *"I can't pay you back, man. That auction is beyond my means."*

"But it's not beyond mine. Just make sure she doesn't go home with anyone else." Dean had shaken the card at him and laughed. *"You'll be one miserable son of a bitch if you don't. Go get your girl, little brother."*

So he'd taken the card and left the house on a wing and a prayer.

Cassie turned to face him, pulling him from the memory. Her hands hung limp at her sides but she rolled her eyes. "Well, congratulations, you surprised the hell out of me."

He leaned up on his elbows, peering down the bed at her. "Have dinner with me tonight."

She stiffened, shaking her head as she crossed to the walk-in closet adjoining the room, disappearing inside. "Sorry. Can't. I have plans."

"Hot date?" He'd thought about this a lot, too, over the last three years. Wondering if she'd started dating again, if some other guy had his arms around her. He had no desire to hear the answer, but the knot curling in his gut demanded he ask the question.

"Maybe." She reappeared in the closet entrance, now wearing a white, long-sleeved dress shirt. The garment remained open, covering her breasts but leaving her belly bare. She arched a brow. "Does it matter?"

Irritation prickled along his nerve endings. He glared at

her. "You know, I'm pretty sure we were both full of shit that night three years ago. I scared you, because for the first time in your life, you felt something. Have the balls to admit it."

She disappeared into the closet again. "I need you need to go. I actually have to work today."

Her comment hit a raw nerve, drawing him up straight. She meant to insinuate, of course, that she had a job and he didn't. He was dating the rich girl. They'd had this same argument one time too many. Cassie had expensive taste. She'd offered to pay for things he flat out couldn't give her. Fancy restaurants requiring things like black ties. Trips to exotic locations. It had always wounded his pride, because it scared the hell out of him. That maybe one day she'd realize he'd never be able to give her any of that and leave him for a schmuck with deeper pockets. He'd sworn he'd gotten over that in the last three years, but even now he couldn't help but wonder—was her date tonight one of those schmucks?

"Low blow, sweetheart, even for you. Have fun on your *date*." He shook his head and sat upright, scooting to the end of the bed.

When he was halfway across the room, she appeared in the closet doorway, eyes wide. "I didn't mean—"

He held up a hand and shook his head. "Save it. Frankly, I've had enough of this. It's the same shit, over and over." He pointed a finger at her. "I'll tell you one thing. He better treat you right, or I *will* find him, and I *will* kick his ass."

He didn't wait for her response but stalked from the room, in large part because he feared saying something else he'd regret. Like telling her she was his, body and soul. He couldn't expect her to live like a nun for the rest of her life. Nor could he blame her for moving on, either. He couldn't expect her to drop everything because suddenly he wasn't dead anymore.

The thought of her with someone else still made him want to hit something. Namely, whoever the jerk was she had a date with. He'd bide his time, though, because he *would* get her back. She cared more than she wanted to let on, and he *would* get her to admit it one way or another.

He couldn't allow himself to think about where their relationship would go after that. It was more than he could handle right now. Hell, it was all he could do to put one foot in front of the other these days.

Once out in the vestibule beyond her front door, he stopped, dug in his pocket, and pulled out the familiar ring. He'd tucked it in there before he deployed. It had been in there so long he felt naked without it. Scratches marred the once shiny gold, and the diamond had lost its luster a long time ago. It needed cleaning and polishing in a bad way, but he couldn't bear to let someone else touch it. This ring had gotten him through hell. When he looked at it, he saw her, lying on his chest the last time they'd made love. That was the night he'd decided he wanted her, all of her, for as long as she'd have him.

Those long, endless days, when he thought for sure his life would end, he'd held on to his memories of her. When the deliriousness from lack of basic necessities like food and water made him wonder what was real, this ring had grounded him. It gave him hope, something to live for, to fight for.

That maybe she cared more than she'd let on. He needed to hear her say the words. Just once.

For now, he'd play by her rules, which meant standing back and letting her live her life, including dating some asshole who probably didn't deserve her anyway.

* * *

"You told him you had a date?" Maddie's drink paused halfway to her mouth. She stared across the small table at Cassie as if she'd lost her mind. Cassie couldn't be sure she hadn't.

She looked down at her own drink, this one a Cosmopolitan, ordered by Christina, and shook her head. Heat flooded her cheeks. Maddie had a point.

"Not exactly. He made the assumption on his own. I just didn't correct him. And technically, I do have a date." She lifted her glass, saluting the women seated around the table, and took a long swallow.

For tonight's girls' night, they'd decided on a club, something fun to take them out of their routines. Pulsing lights in various colors illuminated the long, rectangular room in blues, reds, and whites. A live DJ sat in his booth at the back of the room. People in various stages of getting drunk swamped the space. The dance floor was jam-packed with bodies out beyond their table, all of them gyrating to the upbeat music pumping through the room.

Every single woman seated with her was married. Hannah was pregnant with her and her husband, Cade's, second child. Maddie had admitted she and Gray were trying to conceive. Even Christina and Sebastian were trying, though so far, they'd had nothing but false alarms. Cassie was the only one unattached, the odd man out. Fitting in with an already established group, she hadn't been sure how she'd feel, but none of them treated her any differently. She had to admit, she was enjoying the night.

What she needed tonight was exactly this: other women to confide in. These women had accepted her into their midst no questions asked. She could be herself here and know they'd give her nothing but gentle honesty.

Across from her, Maddie pursed her lips in disapproval. "The first person the guy comes to see when he gets home is you, and you let him believe you're on a date with another guy? You need to tell him the truth."

In the booth beside her, Christina shook her head and sipped at her drink. "It's a tough road to walk, sweetie. I let Sebastian think I dated all kinds of men. Then for a while, I did, in the name of trying to convince myself I wasn't in love with my brother's best friend. Believe me, I understand. Now, though, I can't help but wonder how much time we wasted trying not to feel anything for each other." Christina set her drink on the table. "Tell me this. *Do* you love him?"

Cassie let out a heavy sigh and slumped back against the black leather seats. She couldn't deny that. "Yes."

Hannah, who'd been quiet during the recent inquisition, sat back in her chair on the other side of the table and leveled Cassie with a somber gaze. "So why not spend one night with him? Or even just a weekend? See how it goes?"

Cassie rested her glass on her leg. "I offered. He won't take me up on it. He told me he can't stay all night, but he won't tell me why. And I'm not convinced it isn't for the best. I'm not sure I could handle him leaving at the end of the night, anyway."

Spending a single night making love to Tyler? Yeah. That she could do. Letting him go would be hard, but she'd spent three years wishing she'd had one last time with him. Even simply to lie with him in the dark, to feel him beside her, to listen to the beat of his heart. She wanted it, more than she could admit to herself. Him leaving at the end of the night, though, would leave a wound in her heart. She couldn't play the carefree party girl anymore. Not being able to wake up in his arms after spending the night making love to him would be too painful.

"I've done the whole one-night-stand thing. It was easier than admitting Tyler's death was killing me. Most of the guys never stayed, and I didn't care, but to do that with *him*?" Cassie shook her head. "It would hurt too much."

Hannah sat forward and picked her drink up off the table. A nursing mother and pregnant, she'd opted for Sprite, rather than the rounds of mixed drinks they'd taken to ordering tonight. "Trust me. If you love him, any time spent with him is better than none. Especially after three years mourning him. Despite knowing I'd have to let him go eventually, I didn't regret those two weeks I spent with Cade. Sounds to me like you just need a reason. You just have to decide why you're doing it."

Cassie let out a harsh laugh. "Oh, that's easy. Because I

missed him. Because I regret everything I said to him three years ago."

Christina hooked an arm around her shoulders, giving her a gentle hug. "Then tell him. You've got a second chance now to do the things you wished you'd done then."

Cassie laughed again and lifted her glass, draining the contents. "That's what Gray said." She leaned forward, setting the now-empty martini glass on the table. "There's still the possibility he'll go overseas again, and I'll have to let him go. Face the possibility that he could go over there and die for real this time."

Hannah arched a dark brow. "But you'll have had the time with him. Isn't that better than the loneliness you feel now? Better than him never knowing?"

Chapter Five

Cassie paused on the familiar porch, staring at the brightly colored welcome wreath adorning the black door. She'd been here a hundred times over the last three years. Out of Tyler's "death" she'd gained a friend: his mother. Now, standing there, staring at the door, perspiration prickled along her skin. God, even her knees wobbled. This time she'd come to see Tyler.

Since getting home from the club at two last night, she'd done nothing but lie in bed contemplating the ceiling. She hadn't slept a wink, because the guilt was eating her alive.

Since Nick's death, she'd lived her life bound and determined not to let anyone in, but Maddie was right. Letting Tyler think she'd gone on a date with another man went beyond just trying to keep him at distance and headed straight into cruel. She didn't like the sour taste the notion left in her mouth.

She couldn't help thinking about what Christina had said, either. That this was her chance to do everything she regretted not doing three years ago. Gray and Hannah had told her the same thing. Were they right? Cassie didn't know. All she did know was that she owed it to Tyler to at least be honest with him about last night. She'd see where things went from there.

Drawing her last ounce of courage around her, she straightened her shoulders and knocked on the door. It opened moments later to reveal Tyler. He wore nothing but a pair of baggy gray sweats that hung off his lean hips, leaving his upper body bare to her gaze. Her tongue stuck to the desert dryness on the roof of her mouth. The weight he'd lost over the last three years had honed his body, showcasing the muscle beneath. Where he'd been big and burly in the past, he had an angularity to him now.

It didn't help that his gaze raked over *her*, taking her in from head to toe, or that his eyes filled with a tangible heat. Every inch of *her* came alive beneath the power of his blatant stare. Her nipples tightened painfully behind the lacy material of her bra, because as his gaze met hers again, the memory of the last time she saw him filled her thoughts. His tongue buried inside her, the way he'd moaned and trembled along with her. Oh yeah. Tyler had always loved to give oral sex.

He folded his arms, leaning on the door frame. "Mom's not here. She had to work the early shift at the coffee shop this morning."

She fisted her hands at her sides, determined to stop their damn shaking, and cleared her throat. She'd come over here for a purpose. Fear would not make her back out now. He deserved better from her, especially after everything he'd been through.

"Actually, I'm not here to see your mom." She straightened her shoulders. "I came to see *you*."

He didn't say anything for a long moment but stood staring her down, that unnerving direct gaze pinned on hers. Not a single muscle twitched. "How was your *date*?"

The way the word *date* left his mouth, as if he'd swallowed something sour, had a tidal wave of guilt sucking her under. She stepped across the threshold. Here went nothing. He'd either let her in or slam the door in her face. "Actually, that's partly what I came to talk to you about. Maddie told me I should be honest with you about last night. I've decided she's right."

He straightened off the door frame and dropped his arms to his sides. His jaw tightened and his nostrils flared...right before he stalked away from the door.

"I don't want details. I just wanted to make sure he treated you right." His voice rose as he headed for a doorway some fifty or so feet off to the right. The kitchen, memory told her. "I was about to make breakfast. Want some coffee?"

She closed the door behind her and followed him into the kitchen, coming to a stop in the entrance. Small and rectangular, the space had barely enough room for two adults to stand side by side between the counters lining the two longest walls. At the far end, a large window flooded the space with the morning light. What there was of it, anyway. The thick cover of gray clouds blocked out any chance of sun.

Tyler stood in front of the coffeemaker, the top already open. He pulled out the brew basket and darted a glance over his shoulder, brows raised in expectation. "Coffee?"

"No. Thank you." Her nerves didn't need the jolt right now. She was shaking enough on her own.

He had the nerve to laugh, as if the tension moments ago had been in her imagination. "I don't think I ever remember you turning down caffeine before."

Her stomach tightened. Was he doing this on purpose? Evading the subject in an effort to keep her off balance?

She drew a deep breath, once again drawing her determination around her. "I owe you an explanation."

Hell, who was she kidding? She owed him more than that. If she going to be honest, she might as well go all out.

Her shoulders slumped, dejection weighing on her. "And an apology, I suppose."

His body stiffened. He darted a glance at her, eyes narrowed and nostrils once again flaring as he pulled the old filter from the basket and tossed it into the trash can beneath the sink beside him. "I told you. I don't want the goddamn details. What you do is your business."

A statement that completely contradicted the man who'd stormed her apartment and told her he aimed to win her back. As he moved about the small space, putting in a new coffee filter and scooping in grounds, his movements became harsher, more forceful than they should have been.

She'd hurt him. It hadn't occurred to until right then that she might have actually hurt him with her lies, and the knowledge wounded her.

"You're not actually jealous, are you?" Desperate to ease the tension between them, she said the words with an air of jest, hoping he'd remember the way she used to tease him for his possessiveness.

Tyler didn't laugh. Rather, he froze, so still even his breathing seemed to halt. Several seconds of tense silence ticked out before he did an about face and closed the small space between them in two long strides. He backed her against the nearest wall and set his hands on either side of her head. "You may have thought I was dead for three years, but nothing's changed for me. Every cell in my body still says you're mine."

She couldn't stop the heady tremor that ran through her. Intensity came off him in waves. His jaw set tight, his gaze pinning her to her spot. He stood so close if she but leaned up on her toes she could kiss him. The knowledge did nothing for the need burning in her belly.

Or the dry state of her panties.

Cassie sagged back against the wall. God, he was so damn sexy when he got possessive. No man besides him had ever thought of her as his. It was sad, really. Here she was, nearing thirty, and only one man out of the dozens she'd dated had ever thought her worth more than a good lay.

Tyler didn't do anything halfway, either. Even out in public, he'd made sure any man who even dared look her way knew in no uncertain terms that she was taken. It was in the subtle press of his hand on her lower back as he'd guide her around a room. Or the way he'd pulled her tight against his side and kiss her neck.

Now it made her ache in the most primal of ways. Made her want to climb his body and wrap herself around him.

She shook her head, two desperate little seconds from kissing the hell out of him. "It wasn't what you think."

His direct gaze didn't waver, and her nerves began to tremble in earnest now.

She swallowed hard. "Not what I led you to believe."

"And?"

The hard tone of his voice told her he wouldn't give her an inch, and Cassie caved. Heat crept into her cheeks as shame washed over her. She'd hurt him and for what? Because she was scared?

She glanced off to her left, staring at but not really seeing the still-empty coffeepot. "I didn't have a date with a man last night. It was a girls' night out."

Tyler's gaze burned into her. Finally, he shoved back from the wall and did an about-face. "Why the hell would you do that?"

She heaved a sigh and glanced at him. He paced the length of the kitchen like a caged tiger. Desperate to explain, she shook her head, trying to find the right words. "You can't just march back into my life and demand things be the same. Three years have passed. I—"

As quickly as he'd turned away from her, he faced her again, and the words died in her throat. Tension radiated off of him, his shoulders stiff as he glared at her. He jabbed a pointed finger in her direction.

"I swear, if you tell me one more time how much you've moved on I'm going to…" He let out a low, frustrated growl and spun away from her, dragging his hands over his head and fisting the short hairs on top.

"You're going to what?" She needed him to finish that

sentence like she needed coffee in the morning. Tyler had changed. He'd always been emotional, open about his feelings for her, but since his return, he held back. She could see it in the way his eyes would dart over her face, searching. Now he seemed bursting at the seams.

He dropped his hands to his sides and turned at the waist, eyes narrowed and staring her down. "Fuck you against the nearest wall. Just to prove you're *still* mine."

He marched back to her and crowded her, stood towering over her. Cassie couldn't do much more than blink and breathe. Damn he was sexy when he was pissed.

"While the whole *fucking* world went on about its business, life stopped for me. Time just stopped. How I feel about you didn't change. So, you can't ask me to let you go because *you're* scared. I scare the hell out of you, because I'm the first man to demand something of you beyond sex."

She shook her head in confusion. "And fucking me is going to prove that?"

"Yes. Because ironically, it's the only time you *are* honest with me." His voice lowered, and he reached up as if touch her, but his hands hovered over her cheeks, never making contact. "You always were."

With a heavy sigh, he dropped his hands and turned away from her again. For a long moment he stood, fists clenched at his sides.

That wasn't the first time he'd hesitated to touch her. She watched him go for a moment, the question hovering in her mind. Finally, she decided she had to know. "Why do you do that? You hesitate to touch me."

He stood staring at the window on the far end of the small space. Long moments passed in aching silence before the tension drained out of his shoulders, his fists unfurling. "Because I dream about you."

Now she was confused. His voice came so low, so quiet, she couldn't be sure she'd heard him right, but the dejection and pain hanging on him told her he didn't mean sex.

She took a step in his direction but forced herself not to touch him. Instinct told her that her touch wouldn't be welcome. "What does that have to do with touching me? Dream about me how?"

He gave a slow shake of his head. "I watched them die, Cassie. They made sure we watched and televised the executions. Every single member they captured that day had a family. Johnson and Parker had kids who'll now have to grow up never knowing their fathers' faces. Williams had a fiancée who will never get to see his wedding day. I was next, but I managed to escape. How the hell I did it…"

He dragged his hands over the top of his head again. Cassie waited, heart hammering, not sure she wanted to hear the rest but needing the words all the same. He was sharing something clearly painful. The hurt shrouded him, as if it weighed him down, rounding his shoulders.

A conversation she'd had with Nick once flooded her mind. They'd been seated on the back deck of their father's house in Medina, on Lake Washington, watching the sun set and talking. He'd come home from his second tour in Iraq, where he'd lost friends. Men and women he'd worked and lived with had died when insurgents attacked a supply convoy.

Remembering what Nick had told her that night, it occurred to her where Tyler was right then. He had survivor's guilt. He was the only man to get out alive and no doubt blamed himself.

"I must have had an angel sitting on my shoulder that day, because I took a shot in hell and fought back. We must have tried a dozen times before and it never worked. Hell, maybe it was adrenaline. Maybe it was fear or maybe they were lazy that day. It sure as hell wasn't because I was strong. They made damn sure of that."

Listening to Tyler's quiet words, the images filled her mind. A vivid picture of what he'd been through these last three years. His tall form blurred behind a veil of tears. She wanted to ask how all of that had led to him dreaming about *her*, but she couldn't get the words past the lump in her throat. She'd seen the newscasts, about the way military personnel were tortured over there. She didn't think she could bear knowing they'd treated him that way.

Needing to touch him, she took another step forward and laid her hand against his back. He flinched, his body stiffening, and she jerked her hand back, hesitated, then slid both around his rib cage and up his chest. She pressed her face into his back and held on tight. It made her damn vulnerable. Some part of her brain insisted she'd lose her heart again, reminded her he had plans to go back.

But right then, all that mattered was him. His heart hammered beneath her ear, and he was trembling like a frightened animal. His shoulders began to shake, and just as suddenly as he'd stilled, he turned in her arms. She caught the tears in his eyes seconds before his arms banded around her back, crushing her to him, and he buried his face in her neck. So she tightened her hold on him and hugged him every bit as hard.

How long they stayed that way, she didn't know, but wetness seeped over her shoulder and into the neck of her blouse. He held her so tightly she could barely breathe, but after a while, his shaking stopped. When he lifted his head again, his cheeks were wet, his eyes red. He stared down at her, gaze searching for long, aching moments. She didn't know what to say to him. What the hell could she say? *I'm sorry* wasn't enough.

Some invisible thread apparently holding him back seemed to fray and let go. Cassie drew a shaky breath, desperate to drum up *something*, when his mouth came down hard on hers. Demanding and unrelenting, his kiss fit the moment. God help her, she lifted onto her toes, wrapped her arms around his neck, and kissed him back.

Because he needed her to. And because she needed his kiss like oxygen.

When she gasped into the connection, he dove in, his tongue thrusting into her mouth, restless and searching. When she reached out her own, giving him back everything he gave her, he groaned, an agonized, needy sound that made her shiver and made her chest ache.

His hands slid over her hips to her ass, and he lifted her off her feet, turned them, and set her down on the kitchen counter. He reattached his mouth to hers, another hard, demanding kiss, and let go of her long enough to shove his sweats down his thighs. Then his hands were on *her* thighs, sliding up and around to her ass. He pulled her to him, her skirt sliding up her legs, effectively freeing her. She reached between them and pulled her panties aside, and he pushed forward, driving into her in one long, slick thrust.

He began a pummeling rhythm, hard and fast and unrelenting. She didn't have it in her to deny she needed him. Her body wrapped itself around him, bowing into him as she thrust against him in return.

Their lovemaking took on a frantic, desperate note. The sounds filled the kitchen. The slick push of his cock deep inside of her. His quiet grunts and the soft moans she couldn't contain. She didn't have time to think, let alone remember to breathe. He hammered into her over and over. No doubt he staked his claim, proving he owned her, because he didn't slow down, didn't try to be gentle, but drove deep and hard. Each luscious stroke pushed her beyond her boundaries, bordering on the point between pleasure and pain, but her body responded all the same.

Each thrust hit the exact right spot deep inside. His pelvis hit her clit as surely as if he'd stroked her with his fingers or his tongue. In a matter of what could only be minutes, her orgasm slammed into her. She dropped her head to his shoulder, moaning as wave after wave of intense pleasure tore her apart at the seams. Her fingers curled into his back with the force of it. She had to be hurting him, but she couldn't think enough to make her fingers release.

Tyler didn't complain. He let out another deep groan and

thrust into her one last time, his whole body shaking as he found his own release, emptying himself deep inside her.

Long minutes passed in silence. He clung to her, buried his face in her neck, his harsh breathing hot against her skin. She couldn't let him go if she tried.

When he finally lifted his head from her throat, he pressed a kiss to her lips, so gentle her heart clenched and tears pricked at her eyes. He leaned his forehead against hers and furrowed his brow. "You still owe me a date."

Heart stuck in her throat for a moment, she could only nod. She didn't have it in her to deny him anymore. It would probably break her heart in the end, but the girls were right. She needed this time with him. "Saturday okay? I'm attending a jewelry show this week, showing off some of my new pieces. Between that and the shop, by the time I get home at night, I'm going to be beat."

The corners of his mouth twitched, his eyes glittering with triumph. "I should have just pounced on you the first time I saw you. Would have saved me a whole lot of trouble. A good fucking and you roll over like a contented cat after a bowl full of cream."

She rolled her eyes and smacked his shoulder but couldn't hold back her grin. "Yeah, pat yourself on the back, soldier boy. You always were so damn sure of yourself."

He nipped at her bottom lip. "That was awesome, and you know it." As suddenly as he'd teased, though, the playful light left his eyes, replaced once again by the tender heat that melted her everything. "Saturday works great for me."

Chapter Six

Cassie knocked on the door, then pivoted and paced to the end of the dock. She stood staring out over the water, but the beautiful surroundings failed to calm the tremor in her stomach. Gray lived on a houseboat on Lake Union in a beautiful little neighborhood. Houses like his, in various sizes and shapes, connected by a series of docks that served as walkways, all facing the lake. Any other day, the view alone could soothe a rotten mood. Gray and Maddie had something special here.

Now it did nothing for the churning in her stomach. It was Tuesday evening. A little after 6:00 p.m. and the sun had begun to sink below the horizon. Since leaving his mother's house Sunday night, she couldn't stop thinking about Tyler. He'd left her at the door with a kiss that melted her panties clean off and told her simply, "I'll see you Saturday."

She hadn't spoken to him since, and the thought of their

date had her coming out of her skin. So when today's jewelry show ended, she couldn't resist coming to see Gray. She needed a big dose of his calm wisdom.

The dead bolt chinked open behind her, and she turned. Gray leaned around the doorway, his searching gaze stopping when he spotted her. She returned to him on legs that wobbled more than the dock beneath her.

Right hand on the frame, Gray smiled. "Hey."

One look at his gentle smile and the words pounding around inside of her burst from her lips. "I slept with him."

"Oh my God!"

Maddie's excited squeal sounded two seconds before the door whipped open. She appeared beside Gray, reached out, and grabbed Cassie by the wrist, tugging her inside. Gray closed the door behind her, and Maddie turned, fiery brows rising, her baby blues lit with excitement. "So, you did it. You told him the truth."

Cassie nodded. "We…talked."

Gray moved around her, heading for the kitchen. "We were just making dinner. You hungry?"

Heat flooded her face again. Cassie glanced down at her feet. "God, I feel like such a child. I'm interrupting. I'm sorry. I'm coming out of my skin, and I needed a big dose of your sanity."

Maddie wrapped her in a hug. "You're always welcome here, sweetie. Stay for dinner."

Cassie shook her head. "I don't want to intrude."

"You're not." Gray moved to the stove and lifted a lid on a simmering pot, a thick puff of steam wafting upward. "You got here right on time. Dinner's done and there's plenty to go around. We can talk while we eat."

Temporarily distracted by the warmth and friendship pervading the room, Cassie turned her head, whispering to Maddie. "What's he making?"

Because she knew him. Gray was a health nut. He worked out five days a week. His diet consisted of what he called *clean eating*. He didn't eat anything processed or refined, preferred his food in its purest form, which meant he ate a lot of fresh fruits and vegetables. Gray had been tall and thin in high school, the epitome of the geek, minus the Coke-bottle glasses. Since graduating, he'd worked hard to get himself in better shape. Cassie had always wondered if he'd done it in part to move beyond the awful things his birth father had done to him, but she had to admit he looked damn good. Her and vegetables, though, weren't exactly on speaking terms.

Gray shot a frown over his shoulder. "You and Maddie, I swear. Vegetables are good for you, you know."

Maddie giggled. "He's making spaghetti. Whole wheat pasta, of course, freshly made."

"And garlic bread," Gray added.

Cassie shook her head. "Only you make your own pasta, Gray. Please tell me you made your meatballs."

"Lots of people make their own pasta. It's better fresh. And yes. You know me. Can't eat spaghetti without meatballs."

A habit, he'd told her once, he'd picked up from his adoptive father, Arthur. The man apparently loved to cook and had taught Gray. Gray had gotten his meatball recipe from Arthur. Cassie had to hand it to him. They were divine.

Gray nodded in the direction of the center island behind him. "Grab a glass of wine and have a seat. Tell me what's on your mind."

Maddie took her hand and pulled Cassie into the kitchen. There, she moved to the center island separating the kitchen from the dining room, reached into a cabinet, and pulled out another wineglass.

Cassie moved to the table and eased into a wicker chair. Given he lived on a boat, the house was fairly large, but his décor fit the man. Simple and rustic, but charming all the same. Wicker chairs, everything done in earth tones. The dining room contained a light oak table and dark wicker chairs topped with white cushions. Simple but beautiful.

Maddie poured two glasses of red wine, then moved around the island, setting a glass in front of Cassie. She dropped into a chair across from her and grinned. "So?"

Cassie took a sip of her wine before answering. "I went over to see him. I told him the truth about our girls' night out."

"He wasn't mad, I take it?" Gaze on his task, Gray pulled down plates from a cabinet and began to fill each with a small pile of noodles.

A fierce heat climbed into her cheeks. Cassie averted her gaze to her wine, swirling the dark liquid in the clear glass. "Ooh, I wouldn't say that. More like jealous."

Across from her, Maddie grinned ear to ear. "Oh, I love it when Gray gets jealous. So damn sexy."

"I really should tan your hide for teasing me all the time, you know." Gray shot a frown over his shoulder.

Maddie turned her head and blew him a kiss. "Sorry, baby, but it's sexy." She faced Cassie again and waggled her brows, leaning forward to rest her elbows on the table. "I'm guessing by the look on your face it was fantastic."

Cassie couldn't help the laugh that escaped her. "Truthfully? It was incredible, and as much as I know I shouldn't have, I can't regret it."

It hadn't occurred to her, either, until after she'd left Tyler's house that they hadn't used a condom. The possibility of a pregnancy tied her stomach in knots. She wasn't even sure she wanted kids yet, and if she ever really lost him, she'd be left to raise his child alone.

She looked at her glass, staring into the murky liquid, melancholy rising over her. "I agreed to go out with him. Technically, I owe him, per the rules of the auction, but…"

Maddie nodded, a knowing look in her eyes. "But it's not exactly a hardship."

Cassie sighed. "I'm looking forward to spending time with him." More than she had words to express. She ached even now thinking about it. Where he'd take her, where the night would end. "But I'm scared. If the psychiatric evaluations clear him enough for that job, it means he'll be going back. I know he won't be on the front line, but innocent people have died in this war. Reporters who put their lives on the line for their stories. Civilians in the wrong place at the wrong time."

More than she needed air to breathe, she needed Tyler to stay safe.

"Is it terrible that I hope they won't clear him? That he'll be forced to take a desk job instead?" Just saying the words out loud added to the guilt trapped in her chest. What kind of person bet against the man she loved?

"No. It doesn't. You're afraid of losing him again. That makes you human." Gray picked up two plates off the counter and moved into the dining room. After setting them in front of her and Maddie, he settled his right hand on Cassie's shoulder. "Let it go. Enjoy the time you have with him."

Cassie tipped her head back to peer up at Gray. Truth was, she was terrified. She'd spent three years trying to deny it, but making love to Tyler only served to prove that he owned her. "That's exactly the problem, Gray. I don't know if I'll be able let him go. I don't know how."

Three years and she hadn't managed it, even when she thought she'd lost him.

Gray dropped his hand from her shoulder and folded his arms instead. "Stop thinking so damn much. Stop holding back. Tell the man you love him. Tell him everything you haven't. Because I know you. If the worst happens—"

"Way to be helpful." Cassie rolled her eyes.

He frowned and shook his head. "No, I mean it. If he goes over there and dies this time, you won't be able to forgive yourself."

* * *

Her screams echoed off the walls. Cries filled with agony and terror as she pleaded for mercy between her sobs.

Cassie. They had Cassie. God only knew what they were doing to her, but her screams filled with increased terror, with more pain than the last.

Vile laughter echoed down the hall. The joy in the laugh fueled the blaze burning through him.

"Cassie!" He screamed her name, praying somehow it would help, and hurled his entire body weight against the door. It gave a dull rattle but didn't budge.

Pain reverberated up his arm into his shoulder, and he swore under his breath, stumbling back a step.

Another scream pierced the air, this one filled with an abject terror that his shredded insides. He closed his eyes, his chest squeezing until he couldn't breathe.

* * *

"Tyler, honey, wake up."

The soft, feminine voice called from somewhere beyond, like the wispy call of a ghost. He became vaguely aware of a different room around him now, but no matter how hard he tried, he couldn't get his eyes to open or focus.

"Tyler, honey, wake up."

The voice called again, the familiar sound of it wrapping around him, luring him, but who the voice belonged to eluded him.

"Cassie…"

His voice sounded foreign to him, the word barely leaving

past the lump in his throat. He swallowed and turned his head, tried to pry his eyes open, but couldn't make his heavy lids obey.

"No, honey. It's Mom. Wake up, sweetheart."

This time, a hand gripped his shoulder, shaking him, and his eyes snapped open. A dark shadow sat beside him, the slender figure small and thin. The room had darkened, the light drifting in from beyond the doorway leaving the face cast in shadow. A hand reached out, and the images and sounds snapped into his thoughts, flashing in his mind's eye, there and gone.

"Don't fucking touch me." Heart pounding, his breaths coming in pants, he scrambled backward, desperately scanning the room around him as he tried to make out his surroundings. Where the hell was he? Had they moved him again?

He came up against the cold hard press of a wall. Trapped. They had him trapped. His heart hammered in his throat, the sound a dull pounding in his ears. Dizziness swept over him, panic clawing its way up his limbs.

The hand dropped. "It's Mom, sweetheart. You're safe. You're safe, Tyler. Do you hear me? You're safe, honey. You're home, and you're safe."

Her soft, familiar voice finally broke through the haze. His eyes adjusted to the darkness of the room, allowing him to make out the familiar shape of her face, neck, and shoulders as she perched on the side of his bed.

He sucked in a relieved breath and dragged a hand over his face. "Jesus."

He couldn't stop shaking, and sweat soaked the T-shirt he'd worn to bed, plastering it to his body. He closed his eyes for a moment and drew several deep breaths in an effort to calm the fierce thumping of his heart.

Her soft hand settled over his, where it lay on the bed beside him. "I should have turned the light on. I'm sorry, honey. I didn't think."

"What'd I do this time?" As his heart returned to a more normal beat, he opened his eyes and turned his head, focusing on his mother's form beside him. The light from the hallway spilled into his room, illuminating her from behind.

"You were calling out for Cassie. Were you dreaming about her again?"

He rubbed a hand over his face, his fingers sliding over the wetness on his cheeks. Shame crept over him. He'd been crying in his sleep, like he was a goddamn fucking five-year-old having a bad dream, which wasn't far from the truth.

"Yeah." He dragged in a shaky breath. "I'm sorry I frightened you."

His mother squeezed his hand. "Oh, sweetie, don't apologize. It's okay. I just wish I could still kiss it and make it better."

He heaved a heavy breath. "What the hell am I going to do, Mom? We have a date on Saturday. She wants me to stay. How the hell am I going to stay with her knowing she'll see this crap?"

"Talk to her, honey. Have you told her what nights are like for you? Have you told her about the PTSD?"

"I don't want her to see this. The last thing I need is

for her to see exactly how fucked up I am. I don't sleep. When the phone rings I jump out of my goddamn skin. Most nights, I sleep with the light on like I'm still five years old. I can't stand being in a closed room. Just taking the elevator up to her penthouse makes me claustrophobic. If she sees this crap? God, I don't want to know what she'll think of me then. She'll leave me for sure."

"You don't give her enough credit. She may not want to admit it yet, but she loves you. You have to trust that. It's part of love, honey. If you want to marry her, then you're going to have to learn to trust her with the hard stuff. I guarantee she'll surprise you." His mother rose from the bed and bent over him, kissing his forehead. "It'll be okay. I promise. You'll get through this. Talk to her."

She straightened and turned to leave the room.

"Mom?"

She paused at the doorway, one hand on the frame, and looked back at him. "What do you need, sweetie?"

"Turn the light on before you go?" Yeah, asking was damn childish. He might as well have been ten years old again, but he slept better with the light on.

"Sure, honey."

Chapter Seven

Cassie stared at the darkened ceiling above her. It was Friday night. Although it was past midnight and the jewelry store had been swamped today, she couldn't sleep for the life of her. Her date with Tyler was tomorrow night, and she was a neurotic mess. Her heart had taken a permanent place in her throat.

Her phone buzzed from its spot on her nightstand. Still as wide awake as she'd been when she'd climbed into bed an hour ago, she reached over and picked it up, glancing at the screen. The text came from an unknown number, though the message itself left little doubt that number belonged to Tyler. Reading his words made her smile.

253-420-1763: Welcome to my new phone. :)

Only Tyler would send her a text without explaining who he was. He damn well knew she'd recognize him a mile away. She ought to put her phone down and go to sleep, answer him tomorrow. The part of her still terrified of losing him kept insisting she needed to keep him guessing. Keep up the façade that she didn't care about him. If she didn't care, then maybe it wouldn't hurt so much when he eventually left again.

Except she lacked the desire. The time had long since passed to start being honest, with herself *and* Tyler. He deserved the truth.

Simply seeing his message had her heart tripling its beat, though, and her mind rewinding to their encounter on Sunday. Barely four days had passed, but she'd missed him, in large part because she'd spent three years thinking she'd never see him again. There would never be enough time with him.

Her fingers were punching in a reply before she'd even made the decision to answer him.

Cass: Who's this?

She meant to tease him, but a good thirty seconds passed before his reply came back.

253-420-1763: 2 many boyfriends 2 keep track of?

Cassie bit her lower lip. The awful guilt rose over her again. Damn. Apparently, he wasn't in the mood for a tease.

Cass: Only teasing. Ur just an unknown number on my end. NM. Bad joke.

While she waited for his reply and prayed he'd forgive her for being an idiot, she added his new number to her contacts.

Tyler: Not funny.

Cassie sighed. Clearly, he hadn't forgiven her.

Cass: I said I was SRY.

Tyler: U can make it up 2 me 2moro.

The mention of their date set her heart hammering again, though whether in fear or excitement she couldn't be sure. A heady dose of arousal had her body amped up. She wanted to wrap herself around him, make love to him until she couldn't walk anymore. But could she truly stop at spending only one night with him? Let him go when it was over?

Before she could think of a proper reply, another message popped onto her screen.

Tyler: Ur up late. Can't sleep?

Cass: No

Tyler: Me neither. Want some company?

She wanted to scream yes. She wanted, needed, the solid warmth of his body against her. Needed his cock buried deep inside of her. She ached to make up for lost time by making love to him as many times—and in as many ways—as possible. If only to be as close to him as she could. If she had only one night with him, then she wanted as much as she could get.

Except she wanted more than he was clearly ready to give. She needed him to stay. To wake up in the morning to his warmth beside her in bed. In which case she had to be honest with him now.

Cass: Will u stay?

She already knew the answer, but her heart sank in anticipation of it anyway.

Several seconds passed in aching silence before his reply came back.

Tyler: Baby, I can't.

Cassie closed her eyes, dejection and pain seeping through her chest. It hurt. Of all the men she'd slept with in the last three years, she needed *him* to stay, but he wouldn't. He wouldn't even tell her why. He kept telling her he wouldn't stop fighting for her, yet there were distinct parts of himself he kept hidden. Things he refused to tell her. It had begun to make her doubt again. Was he just toying with her? Was this all just some elaborate revenge scheme?

She pulled up his number and hit the CALL button. He picked up after the first ring, but Cassie didn't wait for him to speak. "I stopped being somebody's plaything months ago. If that's all the good I am to you, then this isn't going to work."

It was a harsh thing to say to him, but she needed him to know. If he meant to hurt her, to pay her back for turning down his proposal three years ago, he'd hit his mark.

He let out a heavy sigh. "You're not a plaything to me, Cassie. You know that."

He paused, silence echoing along the line. Some part of her brain told her to hang up, but her heart hung on his answer, and she could only lie there and try not to cry.

"I still have that ring, you know. I took it with me, and I keep it in my pocket. I wanted something that reminded me of you. When I look at it, I see the last time I made love to you, before I deployed. You were lying on my chest, dozing. That's the night I knew I wanted you. All of you."

His voice drifted over the line low and conversational, as if he were telling her about his day, but the undercurrent of need caught her.

A single tear escaped the dam, and she closed her eyes, trying to breathe through the pain squeezing at her chest. "Then why won't you stay?"

The words left her mouth with far more of her heart than she'd intended to give him. He had her, had her damn heart on a string.

He went silent. For so long she wondered if he'd even tell her. Sex was apparently where they'd become comfortable. She ought to be happy for that. It kept him at the distance she needed. So her heart wouldn't get any more wrapped up in him than it already was. It was a date. A chance to make up for what happened three years ago. But she wasn't ready for more.

Except every time he told her he wouldn't stay, it ate away at her. Any other man, she had no problem with them leaving. If they didn't want to stay, she was perfectly fine with that. Tyler was different. He was the one man who held her heart in the palm of his hands. A man with the power to break it. And here she was, just handing it to him.

Something rustled on the other end of the line, and Tyler drew a heavy breath. "It's too raw. Those three years are all I see now. It's everywhere, in everything I do. Every morning I wake up, it's like I'm still there. You want to know why I won't stay? That's it. Because if I actually manage to sleep, I usually wake up forgetting where I am. When I do sleep, I dream. Mom says I yell in my sleep. The last time she tried to wake me in the middle of a nightmare, I lashed out at her before I realized it was her. The last thing I want is for you to see that. God forbid you touch me and I react the wrong way. If I ever hurt you…"

As his quiet spoken words settled over her, her heart clenched. In guilt. In worry. More than that, though, an aching sadness crept into her heart. Here she was, thinking only of herself, and he bared his pain, shared his demons with her. Clearly he had PTSD. What had he been through over there that he was afraid to sleep? That he didn't trust himself not to hurt her? Oh, she knew he would never hurt her, but clearly he didn't, and the knowledge only made her need him more. She wanted to curl around him and hold him, make him feel safe again.

To show him what she already knew.

To have him close now was like being handed a dream. Her heart wanted to grab on to any little bit of him he'd give her, any tiny little shred of time. Where would that leave her in the end, though? What if he went over there and died this time?

The girls were right, though. If she wanted him to be honest with her, she had to give him the same in return. It's what she decided when she'd gone to see him Sunday morning, right? So the words left her mouth on a desperate need to hear his response. "And I need to wake up beside you in the morning. I need coffee over donuts and a kiss goodbye before you leave."

He went silent, aching seconds passing where only the sound of his breathing filled the awfulness sitting between them. They were strangers again.

"A man needs his dignity, Cass. They took everything

from me. My freedom. My ability to live a normal life. I can't even do my job anymore. The army was my life, yet outside of telling them where I was held, I'm useless to them. Because I can't even make it through the day. Is that what you wanted to know? It sure as hell doesn't make me proud to say it. To have the woman I'm trying to impress know I came back half the man I used to be…they may as well have lopped off my balls while they were at it."

The dejection in his voice cut her to the quick. He bared a wound that stabbed at her heart like a knife. She hadn't expected him to tell her that, and as she struggled with what to say in return, the silence filled with a tension of the wrong kind. More tears escaped, rolling back into her hairline.

"I honestly didn't think you'd tell me that. I…" The right words wouldn't leave past the lump in her throat. Shame rose up her neck, flooding her face with a burning heat. She swallowed hard and tried again. "I was afraid you'd tell me you didn't *want* to stay."

That had to be the most vulnerable thing she'd said to him yet. She might as well have admitted she was in love with him. It meant she'd have to make a decision, a hard one. She'd have to be willing to risk losing him again. She'd only just gotten him back. How could he want to risk his life again? How in the world did she find the strength to let him do what he needed to do?

"Wanting it and what I'm actually capable of are two different things for me right now, baby." He drew a heavy breath. "Believe me. I want it. More than I can tell you. But

I'm afraid to sleep, Cass. I'm terrified of what you'll see when I do. It doesn't change how I feel about you."

"I don't expect you to be perfect, Ty. Maybe it's a selfish thing to want, but I watched you leave me once before. You left and never came back, and I don't know if I'm strong enough to do it again." Another heart-on-the-sleeve admission she probably shouldn't have told him, but he was being honest. Shouldn't she be giving him the same in return?

"I'm coming over." He didn't wait for her reply but disconnected.

She spent the next twenty minutes staring at her ceiling, torn between calling him back and telling him not to bother and unable to deny she wanted the same things he did. She needed to be in his arms. If only because she'd spent the last three years wishing she could. She knew damn well she ought to be letting him go and walking away, but he was alive, and having him standing in front of her was like holding out a sandwich to a starving man. How the hell was she supposed to resist?

When a knock on the door finally came, she pried herself out of bed, heart in her throat as she made her way up the hallway. Her fingers shook so much it took her two tries to undo the dead bolts. When she finally opened the door open, he was standing in the vestibule, hands in the pockets of his sweats.

As his gaze caught hers, his brow furrowed, eyes filling with determination. He didn't wait for her to invite him in but stepped over the threshold, shoved the door closed behind him, and backed her against the foyer wall. He set his hands on either side of her head and leaned down to look her in the eye. "You can run all you want, baby, but I'm not giving up on you. Not a chance in hell."

He cupped her face in his hands and pulled her mouth hard to his. His kiss was encompassing and demanding, as if he had a point to prove, and she couldn't stop the quiet, relenting moan that left her. Neither could she stop herself from melting into the heady press of his mouth or her hands from sliding up the luscious warmth of his chest.

She couldn't deny it. That she needed him. To touch him, to be as close as humanly possible.

There in that moment, something cracked between them. His tongue plunged into her mouth, a tender hot stroke as his hands slid down her sides to her ass. He shoved her pajama pants over her hips, where they pooled at her feet, even as she was reaching down and tugging open the button on his jeans.

"Condom," she whispered, tugging down his zipper. "Tell me you have a condom, Ty."

If she had to wait until she got all the way into her bedroom, she might come to her senses and send him home. Right or wrong, she needed this. This one simple connection. Just to feel him inside of her, against her.

He pulled back enough to meet her gaze, the same raw honesty echoing back at her from the depths of his eyes as he fished a plastic packet from his back pocket and held it out to her. As if he were every bit as lost as she was. It had always been this way with him. Desperate. Hungry. Impossible to deny.

No sooner had she plucked the condom from his fingers than he was lifting her off her feet and pressing her back against the wall. He pinned her there with his hips, his erection settling against her core, and claimed her mouth again.

She reached between them, pushed his jeans past his hips. His cock settled hot and heavy against her mound, and Cassie moaned softly, unable to resist sliding her hand into his jeans to palm his erection. God, her need for him…

She'd barely rolled the latex down his length when he surged forward, pushing into her in one slick, hard thrust. Like that morning in his mother's kitchen, he didn't seem to hold back. It wasn't soft and sweet and slow, the way sex had been before he left for deployment. Instead, he drove into her deep and hard, and all Cassie could do was hang on. Let him take her world and spin it out of control.

Let him make her forget everything else, all the worry, all the fear. Everything but this. His quiet grunts filled her ears, a delicious sound that only ramped up her own need. His scent, clean and warm and all Tyler, filled her lungs with every ragged breath she dragged in, until she was encompassed in and surrounded by him. Until he was all she could see or feel or hear and all she wanted to. Her body bowed into his, into the sweet pressure of his pelvis against her clit and that spot deep inside that lit her up from the inside out.

In what seemed like no time at all, her orgasm slammed into her. Her moan caught in her throat, leaving her mouth as little more than a gasp, as she shook helplessly in his arms. The pleasure swallowed her whole. Tyler groaned from down deep, his hips jerking as his own orgasm claimed him.

They stood that way for long moments, holding each other in the aftermath, their combined harsh breaths the only sound in the otherwise silence of her condo. She didn't want to think about what it meant, for her or for their relationship. Right then, all that mattered was being here. In his arms.

After a few moments, he pulled back enough to look at her, his hands shaking as he brushed them over her face, pushing her long bangs out of her eyes. He kissed her softly, the barest brush of his mouth over hers, then tightened his hold on her bottom and turned.

He paused long enough for her to shove the door closed behind him, and he strode through the apartment, carrying her into the bedroom, setting her down on the bed. He climbed in with her, pulled her against his side, and she reburied her face in his chest.

God help her heart when their date ended tomorrow night.

* * *

The following evening, Tyler lay in bed, staring at the ceiling. The house around him was silent, save the soft whir of the heat blowing. His mother had left an hour ago. She had to work the closing shift at the coffee shop, leaving him to get ready for his date with Cassie. He'd even gone to Dean's this morning to pick up a car. His brother had loaned him his BMW for the evening.

He'd texted Cassie an hour ago, telling her he'd pick her

up at six. At a little after four-thirty, he still had an hour before having to leave to go get her. He ought to be getting up, doing things like combing his hair and getting dressed. What he was doing instead? Lying in bed, stroking an erection. With leisure. Like he was sixteen again.

He'd been lying there, staring at the ceiling, stroking like he had all the time in the world. A stupid-ass grin had plastered itself across his face he couldn't wipe off if he tried. He hadn't had a spontaneous erection in three years. Life had become about getting through the day. For over three years, he'd lived that way. Since he'd been home, getting back into any semblance of a routine was difficult. Sleep had become a rare treat, fatigue his newfound friend.

Today, especially, reminded him how worthless he was. He didn't have a job. He'd come back broken. Oh, he wanted a life with Cassie, but how the hell could he take care of her when he could barely take care of himself? He lived with his mother, for crying out loud. What would he do for work? He didn't have any skills, save maybe repairing his bike, and even then, he hadn't had any formal training. He hadn't gotten good grades in school, either. He was good at being a soldier, but that was all but a dead end now. Stolen from him.

He'd never stop trying, though, because he needed some semblance of normal, and he wanted her. No, scratch that. He *needed* her. She'd gotten him through some of the darkest days of his life. She deserved someone who could take care of her. The sad truth was, though, he wasn't anything resembling normal. What the hell could he even offer her, really?

In the shower, though, he'd gotten to thinking about their date, and for a blissful few moments he'd gotten lost in memories of making love to her. His cock had sprung to life, hard enough to hammer railroad spikes. That fact flat out fucking amazed him. Hell, *she* amazed him. He couldn't wait to see her. He had plans for her. Ones he hoped she'd respond to. He'd likely be hard all damn night, waiting for the moment when he could seduce her out of the jeans she'd be wearing.

He couldn't be sorry for it. He'd barely been home two weeks now, but already she was pulling him out of himself, out of the hell that lived in his head, and he wanted to dive into it. Into *her*.

The little jingle of an incoming text sounded from the nightstand beside him, drawing him from his thoughts. His heart drummed in hope, and his poor cock went forgotten as he lifted up onto an elbow, snatching his phone off the nightstand. A message from Cassie blinked across the screen.

Cass: Where r we going? I need 2 know what 2 wear.

His grin widened. She'd hate what he had to tell her next. He could hear her complaining already.

He punched in a quick reply.

Tyler. Jeans.

Then he sat back and waited. Cassie was feminine to the core. Her closet was full of skirts, and she had more heels than any woman he'd ever known. He loved her in them, but to see her in a pair of jeans would be a treat, if only because she wore them so rarely. She had the finest ass he'd ever seen. In a pair of jeans, her ass was a thing of beauty.

As he'd suspected, her complaint popped up seconds later.

Cass: Can't I wear a skirt? Jeans make my ass look a mile wide.

He smiled. He could hear the whine in her voice. Oh how fun it would be torturing her, keeping her off balance.

Tyler: Not where we're going. & ur ass looks incredible in jeans.

Cass: Where r we going again?

He loved the thought of her over there, in her penthouse, texting him. Was she naked like he was? Just out of the shower and parading around that huge closet of hers in her panties trying to decide what to wear?

His cock twitched against his belly, urging him to ask the question, and before he could make the decision, his thumbs were punching it out.

Tyler: U'll see. What r u wearing?

Cass: Panties and a bra. Y?

Tyler: What color?

Okay, so he didn't really need to know, but he couldn't help himself.

Cass: Black

The vision filled his mind, and he stifled a groan. Damn. He loved her smooth, creamy skin in black.

He flopped back on the bed. Some part of his brain reminded him he needed to get dressed and get over there. They'd never start their date at this rate, and he needed tonight. It went with his plans. He couldn't help himself, though. His brain, what little of it still worked, was in her underwear.

Tyler: Take off the panties

A good thirty seconds passed without a response. Would she turn him down? He hoped not. He'd been right. Focusing on the physical appeared to be working. One kiss and she was putty in his hands, and he wanted her burning during their date.

Though he had to admit she really had changed over the last three years. He hadn't meant to tell her the things he had Sunday morning. She'd gotten to him. He'd dreamt of her again Saturday night. Her showing up wanting to talk about her damn date had pushed him over the edge. He wasn't ready to tell her everything yet, but he couldn't be sorry he'd told her either. Just lying in her bed last night, wrapped around her, had afforded him a few hours of peace. He hadn't slept, and he'd left after she'd fallen asleep, but for those few hours, his head had quieted.

Whatever magic she weaved over him, he wanted to get lost in it.

His phone dinged, announcing her reply, and he glanced down.

Cass: You first.

He smiled. Her response came from shyness, of course. Cassie could be a strong woman when she wanted to be, but when it came to sex, she softened around the edges. He had to admit he liked this side of her the best. Her soft side was a lot more honest.

Tyler: Already there. Just got out of the shower. Take them off.

Cass: Ur naked?

Tyler: Yup ;) Panties, babe. OFF. NOW.

Cass: Done. What now?

Tyler: Slip ur fingers into urself & tell me how wet u r. & don't u dare deny it. I haven't stopped remembering my cock buried inside u all damn day. It's why I'm not dressed yet.

Another long silence. Instead of the annoying jingle of a text, though, his phone vibrated in his hand, her number flashing on the screen.

He swiped his thumb over the green ACCEPT. "Hi."

"You're naked?"

The tremble in her breathless voice pulled another grin out of him. Christ, he couldn't help himself. His heart was lighter than it had been in…hell, years.

"And very hard." He lay back into the pillows and closed his eyes, let his mind fill with visions of her. "I got to thinking about you in the shower, about fucking you on the kitchen counter."

While soaping up, he'd gotten lost in the delicious memories. The sharp prick of her teeth sinking into his shoulder. Her body shaking against him. Her ragged breathing in his ear as he shoved into her again and again.

"You're stroking?"

Her voice came soft, barely a husky whisper. When her breathing hitched, he knew on instinct her fingers were buried inside her heat.

"Yup. And so are you. I can hear it in your breathing. You're pumping those fingers aren't you?"

She drew a ragged breath this time. "Yes."

Her soft admission had his balls tightening. He groaned. "Tell me how wet you are, Cassie."

"Sooo wet. I ache, Ty. I was thinking about you, too, you know."

He allowed himself a leisurely stroke, just to ease the ache, but it wasn't enough. He wanted her. "Tell me."

"I should thank you. For coming over."

"You can thank me later, sweetheart, when I make you come so hard you forget to breathe."

She moaned this time, and her breathing grew ragged and harsh. "*Oh, God.* Tell me how hard you want to fuck me, Ty. Tell me what you want to do to me."

His head filled with visions of her. Lying on her huge bed, legs spread, fingers buried in her hot little pussy. His cock swelled to the point of pain, and each stroke of his hand shot pleasure to his fucking toes. A few luxurious strokes would be all it took to send him over the edge, but he forced himself to stop. "Uh-uh. Don't come. You're not allowed to come, do you hear me? That orgasm belongs to me."

Cassie let out a frustrated groan. "Oh, that's so not fair, Ty. You can't heat me up like that and ask me to stop."

"Trust me, baby. I have plans for you. But I want you hot. I want you begging for it."

She let out a little huff of breath, a relenting sound that had him imagining the look on her face. No doubt she glared at him. "Not fair, Ty. Did *you* come?"

"Nope. Didn't intend to. I was just…enjoying it." He sighed. The answer wasn't pretty. Hell, it wasn't even "manly." Definitely not something he'd admit to his brother.

But she wanted honesty. She wanted in, and at some point, if he wanted her back, he'd have to let her.

He released his cock, the desire gone as his mood shifted, his mind going back to that dark place. He didn't want to go there anymore, yet everything he did or saw or heard triggered something ugly.

He swallowed the fear beating to life in his chest, drew a deep breath, and let the words fly. Sent them out on a wing and a prayer. "Life became about surviving for me, Cass. About living from day to day. To a large degree, it still is. Until I showed up at your apartment the night of the auction, my cock hadn't risen for anything. Up until that night, I hadn't been hard or even thought about sex in so long I wasn't even sure the damn thing still worked. It's a pathetic thing to admit to you. I'm not even sure I want to know what you think. But that I'm hard at all and you're not even here is amazing to me."

He longed to admit *she* was the reason he'd lived through it, but stopped himself. That was enough honesty for the moment, thank you.

She didn't say anything. Not so much as a hitch of breath echoed across the line and his gut tightened as he waited for her reaction.

"Don't you dare come. If my orgasm belongs to you, then yours belongs to me. Got it, soldier boy?"

His eyes popped open, a stupid-ass grin plastering itself across his face. The tightness in his chest eased, and he took a breath, unaware he'd been holding it. He hadn't expected her to say that. He'd expected…judgment. For her to be disgusted with him and hang up on him, to cancel their date. That she hadn't done any of that gave him the sensation of standing on the top of the tallest mountain and made him feel as free.

"You got it. It's all yours. I'm going to rock your world, sweetheart."

"I'm holding you to that, you know." Her voice held a hint of smug amusement, and the tension of moments ago evaporated. "When are you coming over?"

"I'll be there soon. Remember. Wear jeans. You *could* wear a skirt, but trust me, you'll be more comfortable in jeans. And socks. Don't forget socks."

She let out a quiet laugh that lit up his world. "All right. Jeans it is. I'm trusting you, Ty."

"Good. I won't let you down, I promise. We'll have fun."

Chapter Eight

God, she's beautiful.

Standing on her doorstep a few hours later, that was the only thought in Tyler's head. Cassie opened the door and whatever greeting he might have uttered lodged in his throat, lost as he took her in. He spotted a white T-shirt and a beige sweater in the mix, but his gaze was stuck on her jeans. Well worn and skintight, they hugged every gorgeous curve. God bless the man who'd invented skinny jeans.

He forced his gaze off her legs—lest he forget about their date altogether, throw her over his shoulder, and cart her off to her bedroom—and offered a smile. "Turn around."

She frowned. "Why?"

He had to be grinning like a fool at this point, but he felt lighter than he had in a while. Thoughts of Cassie occupied his mind, leaving him blissfully free. He was damn well going to enjoy it. "Because I want to see your ass in those jeans."

A slow grin curled across her face, but she obliged and

turned her back to him. She even had the audacity to wiggle said denim-covered ass. She teased, of course, but every inch of him stood up and took notice.

While some part of his brain reminded him he had an actual reason for taking her out, he stepped across the threshold anyway and cupped her ass in his hands. Damned if he didn't want to peel off those jeans, just to feel her skin. Part her thighs and dive between them. He could spend hours making love to her and never get enough. Skin on skin, with nothing between them but the perspiration they worked up in each other.

Christ. That had to be a record. Under a minute and she had his cock thickening behind his zipper and hunger blazing a trail through his blood. He'd never get through tonight.

When he squeezed her cheeks—because what man in his right mind could resist?—she squealed and giggled, spinning to face him. His arms closed around her of their own accord, and the playful moment flitted away. As his hands reclaimed their hold on her backside, it occurred to him exactly where he was and how he'd gotten there. The panic hadn't come this time. The memories weren't beating down his door. There was only Cassie and the light in her eyes.

Her palms settled on his pecs, warming his skin through his T-shirt, and although she flashed a sweet smile, wickedness glinted in her eyes. "You're in an awful good mood tonight. You didn't finish what we started earlier, did you?"

He settled his fingers in her back pockets, tugging her flush against him. No way could she *not* feel his reaction to her. His zipper pressed painfully against his erection.

"Sweetheart, I've been hard for hours, and it's your fault." He leaned down, caught her bottom lip between his teeth, and tugged gently. "You're in big trouble later."

Cassie's playful smile melted, her eyes growing distant. Was she still having doubts about him? About them? Was she standing there trying to decide if a night with him was even worth it?

He tightened his hold, drawing her in tight. If he couldn't convince her to give him more, he might only have one night with her, but he wanted it all. "We'll negotiate the time frame later. And since you asked, I'm curious. Did *you* finish after we hung up?"

"No. Damn you." She glared up at him, though one corner of her mouth twitched. "I'm throbbing, no thanks to you. I'm not sure I'll be able to sit still tonight."

He grinned, full-out, because damn, he couldn't help himself. If all went according to plan, she'd be climbing his body by the time he dropped her off later. "Yeah, well, good, because so am I. Besides, you won't be sitting for hours."

She wound her hands around his neck and pressed her body into his, pushed her breasts into his chest, and rocked her hips against his. She peeked up at him from beneath her lashes. A devious attempt to persuade him, no doubt. "We could always skip the date and get to the fun stuff sooner."

A quiet groan escaped him. Did she know how much he wanted to do exactly that?

With a strength he didn't know he possessed, he reached up and unwound her arms, took her hands in his, and stepped back away from the temptation she presented. The glimmer in her eyes said she knew how difficult it was for him, too. The little minx.

"No way. If one night's all I've got, you can bet your sweet ass I'm going to make the most of it. And that includes the simple things like having dinner and doing something fun." He winked, then forced himself to release her hands and glanced at her feet. Bare toes, of course. "You'll need socks, baby. And a sensible pair of shoes."

She let out a reluctant sigh and released him.

"Fine. Have it your way, but don't plan on sleeping tonight." She rolled her eyes and spun away from him, but as quickly as she'd turned, she halted. Tension rose over her, bunching her shoulders, and for a moment, she stood stock-still.

He didn't have to ask to know what she thought. The question hung in the air between them, and the heat of moments before evaporated. Tyler tucked his hands in his pockets and waited her out. He didn't know the answer to this question. Oh, he knew what he wanted. Exactly what she did: to spend the night in her arms. He ached, in a way he didn't have the words to explain, to curl around her and hold her until morning came. He wanted to spend every night wrapped around her.

He just didn't know if he could give it to her. At least not yet.

"*Will* you stay?"

The quiet meekness of her voice stabbed at his chest. He hated telling her this, but he had to be honest with her. "Baby, I don't know."

Staying the night with her scared the hell out of him.

What would she see when he let his guard down and finally managed to sleep? Would he dream? Would this be the night he cried out? Or sobbed like a goddamn child? His mother was one thing, but her? He needed what little manhood he still had left.

Long moments passed in aching silence. The kind filled with everything he ought to tell her but couldn't find the words to express. Things he knew damn well she thought, too, but wouldn't voice.

Cassie broke the silence first.

"Your death was hard on me, you know. I have a lot of regrets, Tyler. I spent three years with this ache in my chest, telling myself I should have said it when I had the chance. Except you're not dead and here you are, but it doesn't matter, because you want to go back over there and I can't watch you do it. It's cruel. I know. I understand why you want to, but if you die over there…" Her voice hitched, and she drew a shaky breath, reaching up to run her fingers beneath her eyes. "If you insist on going back, you're going to have to do it without me. I've lost too many people. I won't lose you again."

Tyler stood stunned. He couldn't be sure if he wanted to shout from the damn rooftops or sink to his knees and beg for forgiveness. She hadn't said the words, but her meaning rang clear as day. *I'll be goddamned.* She *did* care, maybe more than she wanted him to know, but she cared all the same.

"Well, if it happens, it won't be for months. They still have to clear me to go. I'm here *now*. I just want to enjoy whatever time you'll give me."

Some part of his brain told him not to say the words. The time wasn't right. She deserved…something more than what he had. Sweet, perfect words. A romantic setting. Right then, he didn't have any of that, but the words fell out anyway, because deep down, he needed her to know. He might not get the chance to say it later.

"I hit a low point out there, Cassie. I'm not proud to say it. It doesn't make me feel like a damn hero to think it, either, but there were times I wanted to die, where I prayed they'd kill me and get it over with. It's one thing to be kept in a cage and starved. Hell, I could tolerate the beatings, the guns shoved in my face. After a while, numbness became second nature. It's another, though, to realize you're the only one left. And I hadn't a damn clue why."

He waited. For her to say something. To admit he disgusted her, because the sick sensation in his stomach told him she had to be.

When she didn't, he dug in his pocket, pulling out the ring. He took it with him everywhere he went.

"You want to know what got me through? You. I kept that ring in my pocket. On those dark nights, that's what I held on to. It kept me grounded. It gave me hope, something to live for, to fight for. When I tried for an escape that last time, they were moving me again. I'd spent the previous night dreaming about *you*. It was so damn real I woke up expecting to find you there."

Yeah. The cold realization of waking alone, knowing he'd likely never see her again, had ripped a hole in him he didn't think would ever heal.

"That's when I decided. If I was going out, if they were going to kill me anyway, then I was going down fighting. Maybe I'd only get ten yards from the compound, but I was going to die knowing I tried to get home. Do you want to know why?"

Her breathing hitched, and her shoulders began to shake, but Cassie didn't move or so much as turn around. He couldn't be sure if he wanted her to.

"Because I had to see you one more time. You want to know why I showed up at the auction? That's it. Because after a while, I started to wonder if I'd only dreamt you, and I needed to see you, to touch you, to remind myself that you were real. Not something my mind had conjured. So, maybe this is the only night you'll give me, but I need it."

He needed this date like he needed his heart to keep beating.

She finally turned to face him. The tears streaming down her face sliced at his insides. "Ty…"

"Uh-uh." He cut her off at the pass, stopping her words before they could leave her mouth, and closed the distance between them. He had no desire to talk about this shit now. For a few blissful moments, the storm raging in his head had quieted, lost in her, and he wanted to enjoy the silence for as long as he could.

Her mouth opened again, but he put a finger to her lips. "I've said what I needed to say. The rest of this crap? This heavy stuff? Stays here." He jabbed a pointed finger at the floor. "We can talk about it later if you want, but not now. I need this, Cassie. I need to get lost for a while."

At some point, he'd have to tell her why, but he couldn't bring himself to do it now. If she cried again, he'd crumble.

She closed her mouth, and he cupped her face in his palms, wiping the wetness from her cheeks. Despite the desperate need pounding around in his chest to close his arms around her and refuse to let her go, he offered her a smile and forced himself to release her.

"Tonight, we're going to have a little good old-fashioned fun. Now"—he dropped his gaze to her pink-painted toenails and forced a smile—"put some socks and shoes on and let's get the hell out of here."

She reached up, wiping the last of the tears from her cheeks, and nodded, then turned and moved through the apartment. Tyler folded his arms, shifted his weight to his right foot, and leaned against the wall to wait. Cassie didn't do "quick." Hell, ten minutes could pass before she emerged again.

He was right, of course. More than a few minutes passed before she finally returned to the hallway. What she wore on her feet had him shaking his head. Boots. Not any boots, either, but knee-high black ones that looked like they were made of velvet or something. They also had four-inch heels.

He couldn't stop his grin. That was her in a nutshell. His spoiled little princess. Cassie never—ever—left the house looking less than perfect.

Tyler frowned and pushed away from the wall. "Oh, for crying out loud. It's not a fashion show. Don't you own a pair of sneakers or something?"

As she came to a stop in front of him, her eyes widened,

shock rolling across her features. "God, no. Sneakers are required for things like exercise, and the only exercise I do is shopping." She waved a dismissive hand in the air and glanced at her feet. "Besides, what's wrong with my boots? These are Christian Louboutin, I'll have you know."

"Oh. Well, that explains it, then." He rolled his eyes. Yeah, like he knew what that meant. He owned two pairs of shoes: his regulation boots, which had worn out a long time ago, and the hiking boots he currently wore. And about two pairs of jeans come to think on it. One to wear and one to wash. How the two of them ever fit together was beyond him.

"You're just going to have to take them off when we get where we're going, Cass." He sighed. He'd have to clue her in or they'd never leave the house. "We're just going bowling."

Her gaze shot to his, dark brows clear up in her hairline. "Bowling? Seriously?"

Yeah, he was taking the most spoiled woman he knew to a bowling alley. He was probably insane, but he wanted her off her game, and he wanted to have a little fun with her. What the hell did people do for fun nowadays? He'd been gone for so long he hadn't a damn clue.

Cassie went to clubs, that much he knew. He'd gone with her a time or two, back when, but no way in hell he could do one of those again. Wall to wall people and music so loud he couldn't hear himself think? Yeah. That was a meltdown waiting to happen. No thanks. Besides, he hadn't been bowling in eons, and it would go well with his plans.

"Yes. Bowling."

Her cute little nose wrinkled in disgust. "Oh, you want

me to stick my feet in those nasty shoes. Shoes a hundred people have worn before me."

This time, he couldn't contain his laughter and offered her an elbow. "Yup. That's about it. Come on, princess. Your chariot awaits."

Cassie moved into the kitchen, grabbed her keys from the island counter and a little white purse she tucked beneath her left arm. She gave an indignant huff and instead of taking his elbow strode past him to a closet in the hallway. There she got out a long tan coat, pulled it on, and strode out the front door. "I am not a princess."

He laughed as he followed her wiggling ass out into the vestibule and pulled the door shut behind him. "Yes, you are. I'm surprised you didn't come out wearing seven-inch stilettos."

"I almost did. Just to spite you." She shoved a key into the lock and turned it. The dead bolt slid home with a quiet *thunk*, and she finally turned to face him. "Are we really going bowling?"

He hooked his thumbs in his pockets. "Mom used to take us on the weekends when we were kids." He hitched a shoulder. "We went in honor of Dad. He liked to bowl, and we always had fun. I considered the usual dinner and a movie, but that's boring. Everybody does dinner and a movie."

Not to mention the thought of sitting in a cramped, dark theater made him break out in a cold sweat. At least a bowling alley had an open floor plan, no small rooms, save the bathroom, and he'd have good memories to ground him.

"Besides"—he leaned sideways, nudging her with his

shoulder—"I'd like to make you a little wager, and bowling's a good game to bet on."

She studied him for a moment. Something thoughtful passed over her face he couldn't quite grasp before she finally arched a brow. "Were you any good?"

The memories rose over him, filling his mind, and he laughed and shook his head. "Terrible. Dean got the good genes, I'm afraid."

Dean had always been the golden boy. Smart, good at everything he tried, and popular to boot. Tyler had always hung with the troublemakers. The ones who smoked, stole liquor from their parents' cabinets, and egged people's houses on Halloween. Yeah, he'd been *that* kid. He'd grown up, of course, had sown his wild oats a long time ago, chose his friends a bit more carefully, but he still preferred his own company. Or in this case, hers.

"Not from my point of view, he didn't." Cassie stuck her chin in the air, strode to the elevator, and punched the button. The quiet whir of the motor filled the silence. When the doors dinged open moments later, she stepped inside and turned to look at him. One perfectly curved brow arched. "You coming, soldier boy?"

The teasing gleam in her eye pulled a chuckle out of him. That look right there would be worth whatever fight she'd give him tonight.

He winked at her. "Not yet, princess. Not yet."

When he stepped into the elevator beside her and the door slid shut, the enclosed space had a sweat breaking out along his skin. Needing something to ground him, he held out his hand from his side, palm up. The question was, would she take it?

She glanced down, stared for a moment, then looked back up at him. Confusion, fear, and desire all mixed in her gaze. Along with a glimmer of something, like a pulse that moved between them: tenderness. It softened the fear sparking in her eyes.

A blush slid into her cheeks, and a small smile tugged at the corners of her mouth, but her fingers slid between his.

They walked in an oddly comfortable silence to the street, where he'd parked Dean's BMW in front of her building. He hit the key fob, and she glanced from the car to him. "Dean's?"

He nodded.

She stood for a moment chewing on her lower lip. Would she voice her thoughts? Before he could ask, she glanced at him again. "What happened to your bike?"

Ah, his motorcycle. He'd bought it as a birthday present to himself when he turned eighteen. He'd saved for years, working as soon as the law would allow him, to get that bike. They'd spent some wonderful hours riding around, Cassie clinging to his back.

"Still in the garage where I left it. Mom said she couldn't bear to part with it. I haven't gone out there yet to see if it still runs. Neither Mom nor Dean know how to ride, so it's just been sitting. Chances are it needs some work before it'll run. Thought about working on it today, but it's chilly, and I figured my *princess* wouldn't want to be cold, anyway." He bumped her shoulder, grateful when she blushed and let out a quiet laugh.

She bumped him back. "I am not a princess."

"Oh, you most definitely *are* a princess. And spoiled to boot." He grinned and glanced down at her feet. "Those shoes just prove my point."

"Yeah, well, you're wrong on this one." She released his hand and moved around to the passenger side, a teasing spark glinting in her eyes as she peered at him over the roof of the car. "I would love to have gone for a ride. I happen to be very fond of that bike."

She didn't wait for him to respond but pulled open her door. The naughty-girl smile she shot him before she climbed into the car pulled a groan out of him. In two seconds flat he was hard again and pulsing behind his zipper. Her delivery was subtle, he'd give her that, but unless he was mistaken, she was remembering the night they made love on that bike.

The memory filled his mind. Parked on the side of a deserted stretch of road, the stars above them peeking out from behind the cloud cover. Her seated in his lap, the short skirt she'd insisted on wearing up around her waist, and him buried inside of her. He didn't remember much else about that night, but he'd never forget the erotic picture she'd made. Her hair spilling down her back, face tipped toward the moonlit sky, eyes closed in bliss as she rode him.

He shook his head but couldn't contain his grin. Christ. It was going to be a long night. A thoroughly enjoyable one, but long nonetheless, because he'd no doubt be hard for most of it.

Chapter Nine

When Tyler slid into the driver's seat beside her and closed his door, Cassie turned her head to look at him. "This wager of yours? I accept."

She'd done a lot of thinking since their conversation this afternoon. If she was going to do this, then she had to go all in, but she had conditions. It was sneaky, really, and had guilt tightening her chest. She'd be pushing him beyond his boundaries. He'd been through hell, but it was time she faced this head-on.

And hell. Who was she kidding? She didn't bowl. She had to put herself out there, though, because she needed tonight. She wanted one night in his arms. To wake up to his gorgeous rumpled head in the morning. Like she needed to breathe or eat or create her jewelry, she needed him to stay. And maybe, just maybe, her idea would put a fun twist on it.

"You don't even know what it is." He grinned, his eyes illuminated and playful. For the first time since he'd come back, he didn't seem weighed down by the things that had happened to him.

She waved a hand in the air between them. "Don't care. I'm game. But I have a demand of my own, should I win. You go first. I know you. You have something up your sleeve. What is it we're betting for?"

He turned in his seat to fully face her. "All right. If I win, you have to spend an entire week with me. Not just this one night."

That immediately stiffened her spine. Okay, so apparently he didn't intend to play fair, either. She lifted a brow. "And if I win?"

"What do you want?" He leaned back in his seat and shrugged, like giving her whatever she'd demand was easy. Like he'd give her anything.

She drew a deep breath, her stomach knotting in anticipation of the denial she knew was coming. "You have to stay. All night."

His easy smile melted from his face, that haunted look returning to his eyes. Several moments passed in silence. When he turned to the console and pushed the button to start the car, she didn't miss the way his fingers trembled. The engine purred to life, and the tension in the small space became a sharp point between them.

In the silence that filled the car, their conversation two days before floated into her thoughts. Lying in the dark, listening to the sound of his voice, low and etched with a raw sort of honesty. As if it cost him a lot simply to say the words out loud.

"They took everything from me. My freedom. My ability to live a normal life."

"To have the woman I'm trying to impress know I came back half the man I used to be… they may as well have lopped off my balls while they were at it."

Guilt tightened in her chest and doubt rose over her. She was trying to be strong, to hold on to her principles, but at what cost? The knowledge didn't make her feel proud, or strong, or independent. Rather, it made her now feel small and stupid. And completely selfish. How could she force him to do something that clearly tormented him so much?

Before she could think of what to say, Tyler drew a deep breath, beating her to the punch.

"Fine. But we're going to have to talk, and I don't want to do it now. Like I said, that shit's heavy and right now, I just want to get lost in you." He finally looked over at her, emotion naked on his face. Fear. Love. Even a hint of the same heat burning in her belly. The intensity in his gaze bored holes in the last of her defenses.

Not that she had many left.

"You make me forget, Cassie."

She turned her head, looking out at the darkened street in front of them. It was six o'clock on a Saturday night. The streets teemed with people and cars, their lights like fireflies illuminating the night. If he could be honest, she owed him the same in return.

"I'm sorry. I thought maybe instead of just being demanding, I'd make it fun. I…" She shook her head and sighed. "I don't know what I thought anymore. Except that I've spent three years thinking you were dead. I just…I need it. For you to stay, I mean. I missed you, you know. I grieved."

She glanced down at her lap, vulnerability rising around her like a suffocating shroud. Honesty might be the best policy, but it sure as hell wasn't easy to bare your soul to the one person capable of breaking it.

"But hearing how difficult it is for you…it just seems cruel. And really selfish." Summoning strength from God knew where, she forced herself to meet his gaze. "I have things I need to tell you, too, and I don't want to do it now either. So, if you don't want to stay, you don't have to. You can owe me dinner or something. You can cook, make me that great pasta dish you make. Because the truth is, I'd give you that week."

She forced an easy smile, but her lower lip trembled, betraying her. She was about to give her heart to him for the second time, all the while knowing she could very well lose him again. It was terrifying and exciting and it had her trembling where she sat, as if all her bits and parts were hanging out for him to see. Like she had nothing left to hide.

But she couldn't be sorry for it, either, because she needed this time with him.

"I said this upstairs, but clearly you need to hear it again." He reached over, sliding his fingers into hers, where her hand lay in her lap. "Baby, I didn't say I didn't *want* to stay. There's a difference."

Baby. From any other man, that nickname always sounded condescending. She usually heard it when a man was either trying to backtrack his way out of getting caught with another woman or trying to persuade her into something she didn't want. From Tyler, the name made her shiver, made her want and need in so many ways. Most of which made her panties damp, because deep down, she couldn't deny she *was* his baby.

He let out a heavy sigh. "You want to know the truth? I'd stay, because I need it, too. To lie in your arms and hold you. So, we're even there." As suddenly as his dark mood came over him, it lifted. One corner of his mouth tugged upward, and he narrowed his eyes, a wicked glint in their depths. "But you're going to have to earn it, princess."

She couldn't resist an answering smile. "And if I lose?"

He grinned, a full-out cocky smile, and winked. "Then you're mine, sweetheart, to do with as I please, for seven *whole* days."

A heady shiver rocketed down her spine, her clit throbbing in eager response. She squeezed her thighs together, more than a little tempted to move his hand between her legs. A little pressure on the seam of her jeans from his amazing fingers, and she'd come all over his brother's expensive leather seats.

"Bring it on, soldier boy." She turned her gaze out the windshield again. "But you better get going, because all this talk has my panties damp. I'm about two seconds from climbing onto that seat with you."

Tyler leaned toward her, his teeth closing over her earlobe. "How about another little bet, hmm? I know how much you love public sex. I remember the restaurant bathroom I fucked you in. Wasn't it an Italian place? We almost got caught because you came so hard you shrieked. And let's not forget you made it to the Mile High Club with *me*. I bet I can make you come in the middle of the bowling alley without anybody noticing. Think you can keep yourself quiet, princess?"

His hot breath against her skin sent a heady shiver rocketing down her spine straight into her panties. He knew her and knew her well, and God she loved that he did.

She drew a shuddering breath, trembling from head to toe. "Ty?"

"Yeah, baby?" He hadn't moved. His mouth was still right there, his voice a low, sexy rumble against her earlobe. If he didn't stop teasing, she was going come, and he wouldn't have to touch her at all.

"If you don't get this car moving soon, I'm going to unbutton these damn jeans, and I'm going to use those wonderfully long, calloused fingers of yours to make myself come here and now. Drive. Please. I've been hot for you all damn day."

He pulled her hand into his lap, settling her palm over the front placket of his jeans. Cassie stifled a gasp. Tyler was hard, his erection a thick bulge that pressed against his zipper. To make matters worse, he tightened her fingers around his length and let out an agonized groan.

"Oh me, too, baby. Feel that? That has your name written all over it. But your orgasm is mine, remember? *I* get to say when you can come."

She couldn't contain her tortured groan this time. The feel of his cock beneath her hand was almost enough to make her come right there, because those words from his mouth had her mind filling with a hot little fantasy. Of climbing into his seat with him and riding that delicious ridge right to bliss. As he'd intended, no doubt.

She jerked her gaze to him and narrowed her eyes. "Drive."

He had the audacity to laugh, a flirtatious, cocky twinkle in his eye, but he released her hand and shifted the car into gear. Cassie tried not to rock in her seat for what little friction she could find riding the seam of her jeans.

When he stopped for a red light, he reached over, sliding his hand over her thigh. "You do realize I'm so aroused right now I'll probably embarrass myself and come the second you sink onto me, right?"

Her breathing hitched, certain parts of her anatomy begging for attention. "Ty?"

"Yeah, baby?"

"I'm okay with that. Hope you had your Wheaties this morning, though, because I aim to have my fill of you later."

Tyler's laughter rang through the interior of the car.

By the time he pulled into a parking spot at the bowling alley in Renton, Cassie was an aching hot mess. If she had to sit still for one more minute, she'd go crazy. She was sure her panties were drenched, because her clit hadn't stopped throbbing. Most of the drive had been a silent one. Tension of the hot variety had filled the car's interior. He'd caressed her leg as he drove. It took every ounce of self-control she had not to shift his hand to the heat between her thighs.

Tyler exited the car, came around to her side, and pulled open her door, grinning as he held out his hand.

"Come on, princess. I'm going to kick your butt." When she set her hand into his, he pulled her into his arms and bent his head to her ear. "I'm going to enjoy torturing you this week."

Once again, he had her right where he wanted her: a hot puddle of goo. His warm breath on the sensitive skin of her earlobe sent more of those delightful shivers racing down her spine.

Drawing on willpower from God only knew where, she pulled out of his arms and sidestepped around him. "I'm okay with that, so long as you make me come. Hard. More than once."

Without a backward glance, she set her sights on the bowling alley entrance and strode for it with more gumption than she felt. After all, if he wanted to play hardball, so could she, if only in part because experience had taught her it would make for explosive sex later. Except his laughter rang behind her, and her knees wobbled with each step. She had a feeling she was about to lose this bet, and she couldn't be sure anymore if that was good or bad.

He jogged into step beside her and slipped his fingers into hers, leading her inside. The place was packed. Couples. Groups of friends. Families with kids. Every lane was full, each face gleaming with the fun of the evening. Thirty lanes glowed with neon. The sound of balls rolling down the alleys and pins exploding filled the room with a deafening din. The lights were turned low as well, black lighting illuminating people's clothing in an eerie glow. White shirts had turned a dark blue.

Four people stood ahead of them, so they had to wait in line. Tyler stood behind her the entire ten-minute wait, his body pressed against her back. He was still hard, and damn the man, he pressed himself into her ass. Hands on her waist, his thumbs slipped beneath the hem of her top, stroking her skin and sending goose bumps shivering from the point of contact outward.

When their turn came, he ordered four games, but with the alley being busy, they had a forty-five minute wait. After paying for their time and giving them his name, he pulled her aside and turned to her.

"You hungry?"

Okay, so being keyed up apparently made her cranky, because Tyler took one look at her face and grabbed her hand, tugging her in the direction of the connected restaurant.

"I'll take that as a yes. Come on. Let's go get a pizza. Maybe if you're a good girl"—he tossed a wink over his shoulder—"I'll give you some *relief*."

Something in that wink and the amused twinkle in his eye loosened her knees. She followed like a lost puppy, happy to let him lead her anywhere for the promise in those words. It was sad, really. She was supposed to be keeping him at arm's length, but she couldn't summon the willpower or the desire. He had her riding a high nothing could touch and looking forward to the moment when he'd tip her over that glorious edge.

The waitress seated them immediately. As Tyler slid into

the booth beside Cassie, the waitress smiled at him. Him. The woman hadn't even glanced at *her*. "Can I get you guys anything to drink to start off with?"

Seemingly unperturbed, he smiled back. "Soda, Coke if you have it, and scotch on the rocks for the lady." He darted a glance at Cassie and grinned before turning back to the waitress. "Better make that a double. And a large deep dish with the works."

The waitress winked, jotting everything down on her little notepad. "You got it."

As the waitress turned away, heading for the bar across from their table, Cassie nudged Tyler's arm. "I'm pretty sure she was checking you out."

Tyler laughed, light and airy. "I doubt it. I'm not much to look at these days."

"Oh, I beg to differ." She slid her hand over his thigh, hard and tense beneath her fingers. So, he wasn't as aloof and in control as he pretended. Good. At least she wasn't alone in her misery.

He looked over at her. His eyes narrowed, warning her not to push, yet illuminated with a heat that seared her from the inside out. Cassie grinned. Christ, she couldn't help herself. She'd forgotten how much fun it was to tease him, simply to sit in the same space with him and see the playful gleam in his eyes. With a single glance, he could melt her right out of her clothes, and the hunger in those blue eyes told her in no uncertain terms that as soon as they were alone, they were going to attack each other. She couldn't wait.

Tyler arched a mischievous brow and released her hand, only to reach over and settle the warmth of his palm over the seam of her jeans. Sitting in the back of the booth, nobody would be able to see them or where he touched her, and he let it rest there, a hot little promise and a warning. "Are you going to behave?"

"Please." She let out a shuddering breath, her eyes drifting shut. Her body was already riding a fine, razor-sharp line, anticipating the luscious burst of her orgasm. It coupled with the knowledge that they weren't alone. Someone could catch them. At the moment of release, someone, somewhere could be looking right at them.

"Good girl. Relax." He turned his head toward the bar and stroked the seam of her jeans, the lightest of caresses. The fingers of his other hand drummed the tabletop. Like nothing was out of the ordinary. Like his wicked fingers weren't setting every molecule of her body on fire. "Remember, baby. Quiet."

She bit down on her bottom lip and nodded. Despite the thick denim covering her, his apt fingers found the exact right spot. He pressed inward this time, rubbing the little knot on the seams of her jeans against her clit. Her whole body lit up like a Fourth of July firework. Pleasure engulfed her, melting what was left her of sanity. Her head dropped back against the seat of its own accord as her mind focused on the strumming of his fingers.

When he pressed again, grinding the knot against her this time, she couldn't stop the gasp that escaped her.

Tyler snatched his hand back.

Cassie groaned and opened her eyes, whispering into the space between them. "Not fair, Ty. You can't keep doing that, teasing me and stopping. It's torture, you know."

He leaned his head beside her ear. "Baby, you do that again and they're going to throw us out of here. And then you'll have to wait, because I'll have to find another alley."

His hot breath on her neck did nothing but increase the ache between her thighs, but Tyler added to it by nipping at her earlobe before pulling back enough to meet her gaze.

"Quiet." This time the word was a hot reprimand that brooked no objections. His intense gaze demanded she obey. "Or I stop."

She reached over, gripping his thigh hard in an effort to root herself, and nodded. Normally, she enjoyed taking control. Tyler had always submitted willingly to her bedroom quirks, had told her once he found it sexy, and it had made for some fireworks. Right then, she'd have sank onto her knees and kissed his feet. She'd have promised him the goddamn moon and stars so long as his fingers returned.

He smiled, sexy as sin and in control, and leaned sideways to kiss the spot beneath her ear. "That's my girl. I'll ease the ache, baby, but you have to do your part and stay quiet."

"Please." She leaned her head against his. To outsiders, they'd look like lovers, or perhaps newlyweds.

He allowed her to take his hand and guide it between her legs. She managed to stay quiet by keeping her teeth locked on her bottom lip as she cupped his hand over her denim-covered mound. Desperate for the release that had hovered out of reach for hours now, she rocked her hips, sliding his fingers along the seam. The thick fabric pushed the softer material of her silk panties against her clit, providing a luscious friction that set her whole body ablaze.

Her gaze went unfocused, the room spinning away from her. The entire time, Tyler planted soft kisses to her cheek, her ear, her neck, occasionally flicking his tongue out to singe her skin.

When he took control and pressed hard, rubbing the knot into her clit, the hot little bubble inside of her burst. Cassie clamped down on her lip, fighting to keep her eyes from rolling back in her head, as pleasure swallowed her whole.

Cool as a freakin' cucumber, Tyler's fingers didn't stop their torment, but continued to rub the seam into her clit. Super sensitive now, the action only served to heat her up again. Fire flooded her veins as another hard orgasm gripped her.

Cassie tightened her grip on his thigh, digging her fingers into the muscle to keep from crying out. She held her breath, her body trembling. She was sure she tasted blood she was biting her lip so hard. The pleasure seemed endless. He was right. The knowledge they could be caught at any moment only extended the pleasure.

As the last of the spasms died away, Cassie sagged against his side. "Oh, God."

Tyler kissed the top of her head, murmuring into her hair. "Better?"

"Oh, yeah." Her T-shirt now clung to her damp skin, and her breaths came rapid and shallow, like she'd just run the

Boston Marathon, but her limbs were deliciously heavy. She leaned her head against his shoulder as the sleepy lull of satiation moved over her. "I don't think I can move, but that was phenomenal. I owe you."

"Oh, I'll get mine." He chuckled and leaned over, his breath hot on her ear. "When you lose tonight."

Chapter Ten

Good luck, soldier boy." Cassie sidled up behind him, pushed her breasts into his back, and slid her hand over his ass, letting it rest there.

In two seconds flat, Tyler's cock was swelling behind his fly. Standing at the end of the lane, a twelve-pound ball in his right hand, he couldn't help but laugh. They were two games in, and that was the fourth time in the last hour and a half she'd done something similar. Last time, she'd swatted his ass. The time before that, she'd kissed him, pushed her tits into his chest, and thrust her tongue into his mouth. The little minx clearly attempted to throw him off his game.

Damn her, it worked, too. She'd sent his ball shooting off into the gutter three times now, because he couldn't concentrate worth a damn. His mind was currently in her jeans. Namely, on getting her back to her penthouse and out of them.

He turned his head and tried for a glare, but the wicked

gleam in her eyes made his heart pound, and the corners of his mouth twitched. "I see what you're doing, you know. You're trying to sabotage me. That's cheating, princess."

"Just improving my odds." The spoiled brat didn't even have the decency to look guilty. She winked at him, all sassy and full of herself. Christ she was beautiful when she looked at him like that.

"Yeah, you just wait. I'm still ten points ahead of you." He faced the lane again, and she moved back to give him room. Ignoring the heat of her stare, he took aim and swung his arm back.

"Want to know what I plan to do to you if you stay tonight, Ty?"

Her voice sounded behind him as he released the ball, and his hand jerked as possibilities bombarded his mind. All the delicious ways he wanted to make love to her. Against the wall in the foyer, to take the edge off, like they had last night. Or maybe she'd fall to her knees and take his cock in her small, hot mouth…

The damn ball left his hand with a little more force than necessary. It hit the first pin and barreled through, knocking down the six pins in the center and leaving him with a four-six-seven-ten split. Damn it.

He groaned. He'd never make that.

As he headed for the ball return, he shot her a glare. "Two can play at that game, baby. Wait until it's your turn."

The ball came rolling out of the return with a quiet whir of the motor, and he grabbed it and moved to the end of the lane again. He lined up his sights, the way Dean had shown him. His brother had told him once how to do this, to hit the pins right in order to pick up a spare. Not that he'd ever managed to accomplish it.

As it turned out, he managed to knock down three of the remaining pins, leaving one standing, as if to mock him.

Cassie pranced to the ball return with a self-satisfied smirk. "Nice try."

After grabbing her ball—pink of course—she moved to the end of the lane. Tyler followed, moving to stand behind her. He tucked his thumbs in his pockets and leaned his head beside her ear. "Want to know what I want, baby? I want to bury my face between your thighs and suck on your clit. I want to feel your hands grip my head and your hips arch into my mouth because you can't help yourself. And more than anything, I want to feel you come on my tongue."

She drew a shuddering breath that damn near made him drag her off to the bathroom, hiked her chin, and darted a glance over her shoulder. "Are you going to move back so I can take my turn or what?"

"Oh, my bad." He held his hands up in surrender and backed away from her.

Cassie, of course, didn't need his help to ruin her game. Her way of throwing the ball was to hold it in both hands and swing it between her legs. If she wanted to play dirty, though, so could he.

Just as she took her swing, he called out to her. "Good luck, my tasty little treat."

When her ball skittered off into the gutter, he resisted the urge to gloat.

Cassie turned and glared at him, marching back to the ball return. "Oh, it's on, Benson. It's on."

He dropped into a plastic chair and winked at her. "Consider that challenge accepted, princess."

As she stepped up to the lane again, he should've tossed another cocky taunt at her, some barely disguised innuendo, but he could only watch. Despite her protests regarding bowling, they were having a good time. His head had been quiet so far. Not once in the last hour and a half had he thought of that fucking cell in Iraq. The crowd around him, the deafening noise, hadn't triggered anything ugly, because he was lost in her, in keeping her smiling and laughing.

By the fourth game two hours later, they both played so lousy he laughed every time he stepped up to the lane. Cassie, though, was ahead by five points. This game would decide who won his little bet.

As it turned out, his ball curved off into gutter. Leaving all ten damn pins still standing.

Cassie let out a victorious squeal behind him, meeting him at the ball return with a grin plastered across her face and her chest puffed out with pride. She stepped into his personal space and poked him in the chest. "You. Are. Mine. I won, fair and square, soldier boy."

He leaned down and touched his nose to hers. She might have won, but he could still pull a few punches of his own. "I've always been yours. Believe me, princess, I'm going to enjoy letting you have your way with me."

That got her. Cassie froze, heat flaring in her eyes. A heady shiver moved through her as she stared up at him. "So, what now?"

"Well, that depends on you, but"—he leaned his head beside her ear and lowered his voice—"I'm dying to peel you out of those jeans."

Her breathing hitched. When he met her gaze again, she stared at him for one tension-filled moment, grabbed his hand, and marched off, tugging him behind her. He followed in silence out of the bowling alley and into the quiet of the night. She didn't say a word or even turn to look at him as she led him to where his brother's car was parked at the back of the lot. Once there, she pressed him against the driver's door. Hands braced on his chest, she lifted onto her toes and captured his mouth, all fire and determination. She pushed her tongue inside, her kiss hot and desperate, and he was pretty sure they were both shaking.

As suddenly as she'd kissed him, she released him, pausing a moment to catch his gaze. Hers was filled with the same need that had him tongue-tied. Then she moved around to the passenger side of the car.

His fingers shook as he dug his keys from his pocket and hit the fob. Once the doors unlocked, she climbed inside. When he got in after her, she reached over and threaded her fingers with his. "You should get this car moving, because in about two seconds, I'm going to climb into that seat with you. I need you. I…"

She shook her head, glancing over at him, vulnerability rising in her eyes.

She didn't have to say the words. What she meant hung in

the air, igniting a solar flare between them. She needed what he needed. Something soft and slow. A complete meshing of bodies. He had a feeling they really wouldn't be sleeping tonight. Not out of physical need, but the soul-deep desire to be as close as possible. To make up for lost time. Three years apart was a lifetime, and the need in her eyes, mixing with the tears hovering at the edges of her lashes, told him she thought something similar.

He squeezed her fingers, then pushed the button to start the car and moved their combined hands to the gearshift. "Me, too, baby. Me too."

By the time they made it to her penthouse, a tense silence had risen between them. Cassie was unusually shy and quiet. On the elevator ride up, she held herself stiff beside him, hands fisted at her sides. She didn't say so much as a word, and he let her have her space. He knew her enough to know that when she was ready, she'd voice whatever was on her mind.

Every once in a while, though, her gaze would flick to him. The hunger in her eyes made his cock ache. Standing behind her in the vestibule, watching her unlock her front door, he could have cut the tension with a knife. Tonight was different somehow, like they were letting down walls between them.

He found out as soon as he closed her front door behind him. Cassie turned to him, and although she gave him a sweet smile, he didn't miss the anxiousness dancing in her eyes. "You were right, you know. I had a good time."

"Told you." He winked, hoping to see her smile. The

laugh she let out, however, sounded forced. He stroked her cheek with the backs of his fingers. "All right, I can't stand it anymore. You've been quiet since we left the bowling alley. Care to tell me what's going on in that mind of yours?"

She stared at him for a moment before drawing a breath. "I've been thinking."

He dropped his hands, hooking his thumbs in his pockets. "And what'd you come up with?"

"I know I won fair and square, but…" She looked down at the floor for a moment before meeting his gaze again. "I meant what I said. You don't have to stay."

Ah. So that was the reason for her silence. Before he let her off the hook, though, he had to know. "Care to tell me what made you decide this?"

She dropped her gaze to his chest and reached out with tentative fingers, stroking her palm over his pecs.

"I realized I didn't care anymore. I was thinking about it, on the way up. If spending the night is too hard for you, then I don't want it. Because that matters to me, too. That you're comfortable with this, with me." She opened her mouth as if to say something, paused, drew a deep breath and blew it out. "If you could just hold me until I fall asleep? Like last time?"

If ever he had a doubt about whether or not to stay, those words sealed the deal. That she'd give up on the one thing she needed most made the decision a cakewalk. He'd stay, because she needed him to and because he needed *her*.

He closed the distance between them and cupped her cheeks in his palms. "For the record, I *want* to stay. Somewhere deep down, you have to know that. I'm not avoiding *you*."

She nodded but worry still edged her eyes, and the soft vulnerability playing there only reminded him why he'd fallen for her in the first place. When push came to shove, Cassie's *I don't need anybody* façade came tumbling down around her. Deep down, she had a soft heart.

He sighed and stroked her cheek with the backs of his fingers. "It means we're going to have to talk. You're going to need to know what to expect, but telling you won't be easy for me. I'm not sure I could handle watching your expression when I say the words. You're going to be thinking about everything, and I don't want to see the reflection of it in your eyes. I don't want to remember right now. I had a great time tonight. For the first time in a long time, I haven't thought about being over there, and I don't want to ruin that. I just want to enjoy you."

He leaned in, unable to resist stealing a taste of her. The mere mention of the conversation had his shoulders tightening to the point of pain. He'd have to tell her things he'd hate saying to her, and he'd have to watch the emotions she'd try but fail to hide move across her features. Although some part of his brain insisted she wouldn't judge him like that, the thought of finding disgust in her eyes made him sick to his stomach. He'd come back from hell feeling like half a man, and he still feared seeing an echo of the same in her gaze.

But he was willing to take the risk. For her. Because she was the only person he trusted to share this with.

"You've had me wound like a top for hours. I want inside you, baby. We can talk later." He forced a grin, determined to rid them of the unbearable heaviness hanging over them. "Now kiss me, damn it."

Her relief was palpable. Her features lit up like the sun, her grin blooming in her face. A wicked glint entered her eye that made his cock ache. Bracing her hands against his chest, she turned him, pressed him back against the foyer wall, and leaned up on her toes. The ferocity with which she seized his mouth pulled a groan out of him. Christ he loved this side of her. Cassie was taking no prisoners.

Her kiss wasn't soft or slow, either, but fire and seduction. Her lips played over his, her tongue sliding along his lower lip and pushing inside. She had the nerve to tease him, her tongue flicking out and tapping his, only to skirt away when he reached out in return. When she had him shaking with need and completely at her mercy, she went in for the kill shot. Her soft hands burrowed beneath his shirt, sliding over his pecs as her thumbs flicked his nipples.

A deep groan vibrated out of him. Unable to stand her teasing anymore, he cupped her head in his hands and took back control. He deepened the kiss, giving her everything she gave him, and slid his hands to her ass, pulling her legs off the floor. He turned, pressed her back against the wall, and rocked his aching cock against her core.

Cassie dropped her head back against the wall and closed her eyes. Her perfectly polished nails dragged over his shoulders as she arched against him. "If I were wearing a skirt, you could already be inside me, you know."

Already breathless, she found a primal rhythm, grinding against the bulge in his jeans. When she gasped and began to tremble in his arms, he knew she was close.

He groaned and forced himself to pull back. Oh, he had every intention of driving her out of her freaking mind tonight, but he was wound tight, like a grenade without a pin. If she didn't stop, he'd come in his damn jeans, and this time when she went, he wanted to go with her.

So, he dropped her legs to the floor and stepped back.

"Hey." Cassie opened heavy-lidded eyes, a lazy grin curling across her face. "I was enjoying that."

"I know, but any more and I'm going to come with you, and I'd rather be inside you when I do. You got relief earlier. I, however, am pretty sure my balls are blue." He winked and took her hand, leading her in the direction of her bedroom on the other side of the apartment. "Come on, princess. I want to peel you out of those jeans."

Behind him, Cassie giggled, a girlish sound that made him smile again in spite of himself. "I'm going to enjoy watching you come apart, soldier boy."

He waited until they'd entered her bedroom before answering her, using the purchase of her hand in his to pull her into him. He nipped at her bottom lip. "I just bet you will."

That mischievous gleam returned to her eyes as she braced a hand against his chest and shoved. He stumbled back a step as Cassie dropped onto the edge of the bed and held one booted foot out to him. "Pull."

Tyler couldn't help the stupid grin plastering itself across his face. Oh, he liked this game. Cassie, in dominatrix mode, could rock his whole damn world. So, he put on his best submissive and gripped her foot in his palm. "Yes, ma'am."

He tugged the first boot off, tossing it over his shoulder.

Cassie drew her brows together and peered around him. "Those were expensive, you know."

"Yes, but they're currently in the way of me getting those jeans off you." Okay, so maybe his best submissive wasn't very good. Tyler held out his hand. "Next foot, please."

Heat flashed in her eyes as she obliged, holding out her right foot. When he tossed that one over his shoulder, too, she glared at him, but the corners of her mouth twitched. Determined to get her out of those jeans as soon as possible, he approached the bed, but Cassie shook her head and stood. Hands sliding onto his hips, she turned him back toward her, reversing their positions, and pushed his chest again. He dropped onto the edge of the bed and leaned back on his elbows. Whatever her game, he was happy to play. Her hot gaze rooted to his as she gripped the hem of her sweater and pulled it up over her head. One corner of her mouth quirked as she tossed it over her shoulder with her boots. Her T-shirt went next, tossed with a la-de-da style.

Her hands dropped to the top button of her jeans, popping it free. Rather than making quick work of those jeans, however, Cassie began to dance, her hips doing erotic figure eights as she pulled down the zipper tooth by fucking tooth. She turned her back to him, swaying her tight little ass, and tugged the denim down only enough to reveal the top of sheer black panties. Two seconds later, she pulled them back up and continued to dance, running her hands over her body. Up her sides and along the edges of her breasts. Down her stomach to her mound. Then back up to cup her breasts in her palms. Everywhere he ached to touch.

By the time she finally flicked the clasp on her bra, he was pretty sure he was drooling. She had him right where she no doubt wanted him, at her beck and call. She didn't, however, take her bra off or turn around.

He let out a frustrated groan and flopped back on the bed. "Blue, Cassie. They're blue. So not nice to tease me right now."

Okay, so her tactic was freaking brilliant. She had him by the balls, and she knew it. He'd give anything at this point for her to shuck the rest of her clothing and join him on the bed. Hell, he'd settle for the jeans. He could work around the panties.

Something soft landed on top of him, and he opened his eyes. Her bra—also black—lay across his chest. The little minx.

He lifted his head to find her grinning at him, hands massaging her breasts, fingers pinching her nipples. Clearly, she enjoyed his torment.

He pulled himself upright, leaned his elbows on his knees, and narrowed his gaze at her. "In about two seconds, princess, I'm going to pounce on you. I'm going to peel those jeans off you myself, and I'm going to fuck you so hard your headboard's going to leave marks on your lovely blue walls. Jeans. Off. Now."

She released her breasts, held her hands out from her sides, and arched a brow, an invitation and challenge all rolled into one hot little smirk. "Take your best shot, soldier boy."

"Tease." This time, he couldn't stand it and surged off the bed, lunging at her.

She squealed and giggled, backing away, but he followed and scooped her off her feet.

He turned and tossed her giggling ass onto the bed, then crawled up after her, kneeling between her thighs.

"Remember. You asked for it." He made quick work of her jeans and panties, tugging them over her hips and down her legs before tossing them off the side of the bed. He didn't give a flying rat's ass where they'd landed, but something *thunked* as it hit the floor. Gaze set on hers, he crawled up her body, holding himself over her. "If you move, I'll turn you over and redden that ass."

He brushed a kiss across her mouth and pushed off the bed, pulled a condom out of his back pocket, and set it on the nightstand before shucking his own clothing. It didn't help the process move any faster with his hands shaking and his blood roaring between his ears. Neither did it help that Cassie spread her thighs like a sweet invitation and slid a hand over her mound. She strummed her clit with the tip of a finger, watching him through hooded eyes.

When he finally rejoined her, covering her body with his, she let out a dreamy sigh and wrapped herself around him. Her warm hands slid up his back, gathering him closer, and her heels hooked over his calves. "God, I missed this. The feel of you on top of me, your warm skin."

Her words came out on a breathy whisper, but the emotion behind them, the absolute bliss on her face, got him. Yeah. He'd missed this, too. The simple things, like making love to her.

He reached up, tracing the shell of her ear, amazed and grateful he'd gotten his wish. Sitting in that cell in Iraq, thinking his life would end, his last wish was to see her one more time. Now he had her for the foreseeable future, and he intended to make the most of his time with her. "Me too."

She opened her eyes, peering up at him. The familiar connection pulsed between them. It amazed the hell out of him to see the reflection of it in her gorgeous gaze. It was still there, that certain something pulling them together like the moon to the earth. She could put on a brave face all she wanted, but here, with nothing but skin and moonlight between them, she couldn't hide. Everything she felt was naked on her face.

"I missed you, Ty."

Her whispered words were a silken caress, wrapping around his heart. God, she had no idea how much he needed to hear them.

"Me, too, baby." He bent his head, brushing a kiss across her mouth. "So much."

He left her long enough to grab the condom and roll it on, then tucked her beneath him again. Her lashes fluttered, eyes closing in bliss as he slid into her in one slow thrust.

For a moment, he could only stay there, enjoying her tight slick heat wrapped around him. He really had missed this, and as ramped up as he was, he wanted to make it last as long as he could. He wanted to make her moan and sigh, to take her world and spin it beyond her imagination. In large part because she was the light that illuminated his.

Her hands slid down to his back to cup his ass, and she arched against him, working her hips in slow circles, making him slide inside her in miniscule increments. The short strokes drove him out of his mind, because it was what he needed right then. Tender and achingly slow. The soft purring emanating from her throat didn't help him keep a tight rein on his control. Hearing her pleasure only ramped up his.

Shaking all over now, he bent his head, following the line of her jaw. What he wanted was to plunge into her, hot and hard, to drive her past her boundaries and beyond, but he needed to take this slow. He wanted her to come so hard she forgot to breathe.

Because staring into her eyes, the ugliness rose over him, staring him down with beady, red little eyes. Too many nights in that dank cell in Iraq, listening to Williams's screams, had left their mark on his soul. If Cassie screamed when she came, he'd ruin the moment.

He bent his head, immersing himself in the taste of her skin and the glorious scent of her perfume. "I need you to do something for me, okay?"

When he arched against her, pushing in deeper, her nails curled against his skin. She moaned, long and low, her voice breathless and distracted. "*Oooh*. Anything."

He swallowed hard, some part of him clenching tight. God, he hated this. "Don't scream."

She froze, becoming so still he could feel her question even before it left her mouth. "Why?"

A simple, single word, spoken on a soft voice filled with sudden alarm. Exactly what he hadn't wanted. He'd tried not to spook her, but how the hell could he not?

He couldn't look at her when he answered. He had no desire to know what would play in her eyes, the judgment his mind expected to be there. So he concentrated on the spot where her neck met her shoulder. She always dabbed a bit of perfume there, and he let it fill his senses. "Because if you do, I'll probably come out of my skin."

She shoved against his shoulders, turning her head in an attempt to catch his gaze. When he wouldn't budge, she wrapped her arms around his shoulders and buried her face in his throat. "Tell me why, Ty."

The worry and aching concern in her soft voice made his gut ache.

"Not now. After. I promise. Just…" Damn. She deserved the truth, not his constant sidestepping, but he couldn't tell her now or he'd ruin the moment. When he lifted his head, though, her gaze held exactly what he'd hoped not to see—worry. "Just please don't scream. Bite me if you have to, but don't scream."

Aching seconds passed in silence. He could only watch her eyes and wait. He was pretty sure he was shaking for all the wrong reasons.

Cassie cupped his cheeks in the palms of her hand, stroking his skin, her eyes searching for something in his. "What did they do to you?"

Her soft words hit that sore spot inside, and the hurt and guilt he'd barely held in check rose over him. He dropped his head to her shoulder and gave in to the pull of her. The concern in her eyes leveled him. He'd always been afraid that seeing pity in her eyes would leave him feeling…like less of a man. Despite knowing how irrational it was, he'd fear *she* thought of him that way.

To see genuine concern there instead filled him with a relief so profound he wanted to drop to his knees and weep in her lap. To know she accepted him, broken parts and all…God, he needed her. He needed that care. From her. He wasn't sure he had the words to tell her what that meant.

"Not now, baby, please? I just need you. I need to hear the huff of your breathing in my ear, to feel you tight around me. I need you to use my body, the way you used to, grind yourself against me and fuck me like you own me. Because you do, you know. You own me, baby. I'm yours. I just want to get lost in you for a while."

She lay so still beneath him he worried he'd ruined the moment, and seconds ticked out in uncomfortable silence. When he was sure the tension would snap, she drew a breath and sat up, rolling him onto his back. Sitting astride him now, she caught his hands, threaded their fingers, and pinned his arms above his head. She began a torturous rhythm, sinking and grinding against him. Her hot, harsh breaths blew against his mouth so that he took every one with her and everything but her eyes fell away.

He gave himself over to her, to the incredible pleasure she sent rippling through him. She sank onto him with aching slowness, only to rise up, leaving just the tip of him inside, and doing it again. Quiet little moans rolled out of her. Her breasts swayed against his chest, tight nipples grazing his skin to drive him out of his mind.

When her thighs began to shake against his sides and she closed her eyes, he knew her orgasm was close.

He tightened his grip on her fingers. "Let it go, baby. Come for me. I need to watch you come apart. I'm yours, Cassie. All yours. Let it go."

She let out a tortured moan, clamped her teeth down on her bottom lip, and increased her tempo. With every flick of her hips, she sank onto him hard, taking him in one slick thrust. Until she was panting, her headboard repeatedly thumping the wall.

Half a dozen hard thrusts, she went still, sucked in a gasping breath, and ground herself against him, her body jerking over him. Her inner muscles clamped down around him, massaging his cock, and he couldn't hold back anymore. His orgasm rushed over him. He gripped her fingers tight, gasping and shaking along with her.

When the spasms dwindled to tiny tremors, Cassie sucked in a sharp breath and dropped onto his chest like a puppet whose strings had been cut. Still breathing hard, she released his hands and tucked her damp forehead into the curve of his neck.

Overwhelmed by the moment, by her, he wrapped his arms around her, crushing her to him. "I love you."

Christ. He laid all his cards on the table by telling her that. He didn't expect her to say the words back, but they demanded to be heard. Given their heart-to-heart in the car, he had no idea where their relationship was going at this point. He only knew one thing: he needed her to know nothing had changed for him. She had all of him.

Seconds ticked out, an aching silence filled with a palpable tension. His muscles tightened in expectation of the denial. For her to get up and put some distance between them.

Cassie slid her hands beneath him, wrapping her arms around him. Her voice came muffled from his throat. "I love you, too."

Chapter Eleven

Cassie's heart hammered as she waited for Tyler to say something. Some part of her said she shouldn't have told him that, that it was too soon. That she was learning to swim by diving into the deep end. But the truth was, she did love him. Always had.

She couldn't deny the moment staring her in the face, either. She was with him tonight, in part, to tell him all those things she regretted not telling him three years ago. That he was important to her, too, that he wasn't just a fling she could toss aside when she was done. And how much she regretted pushing him away in the first place.

Tyler went so silent she feared he'd fallen asleep. That would be her luck, wouldn't it? She'd finally worked up the courage to say those words to him, and he wasn't awake to hear them.

Except the longer she lay there, the more his body tensed beneath her, so she drew a deep breath and kept going. If she was walking that road, she might as well go for broke. There wasn't much to lose at this point. She couldn't lie to him anymore, and besides, she owed him the truth.

"I'm sorry."

The warmth of his palm stroked down her back, his voice an intimate hum in her ear. "What for?"

"All those awful things I said to you three years ago. I didn't mean them."

His stomach muscles bunched as he lifted his head to kiss her shoulder. "Me too. Sorry for the things I said back then. I was hurt and lashing out."

She snuggled farther into his neck. "You're tense, Ty, and it scares me. What are you thinking?"

"A million different things. Questions you probably don't want to answer right now."

He didn't have to ask. Instinct told her what his question was. He wanted to know where their relationship went now. She blew out a heavy breath and slid into the space beside him, tucking one arm over his bare belly and laying her head on his shoulder.

"I don't know. That's the answer to the question you're not asking. I'm afraid to think about it, because it means risking losing you. And I know that doesn't make sense. I mean, I lose you anyway if you decide to walk away from this, that you're tired of waiting. It's irrational, but the fear is still there. Somewhere inside I thought if I refused to face it, you'd be safe." She lowered her voice, her cheeks heating with the guilt and shame rising over her. God, it sounded so stupid, but in the end, it amounted to one thing. "I would never survive if I lost you for real."

And there it was. The secret she held closest to her heart and the last skeleton in her closet. That she loved him so much her world would crumble—and had—if he ever really died. He had all of her now. She'd finally allowed herself to be vulnerable with him in a way she never had before he deployed.

She sighed and shook her head. "God, you must think I'm so stupid."

Tyler rolled toward her, wrapped his arms around her, and drew her into his chest, kissing the top of her head. "There were points where I thought I'd only imagined you. I'd wake up sometimes with the disappointment of not finding you beside me. There at the end, I'd given up hope of *ever* seeing you again. So seeing you at the auction was a surreal moment for me. It wasn't until I kissed you that it became real, that I knew I was really home." He leaned his forehead against hers. "I can't lose you again, either."

She kissed the center of his chest and closed her eyes, inhaling the scent clinging to his skin. Clean and masculine and all Tyler. "I need to take this one day at a time. The question is, are you okay with that?"

He kissed her forehead this time, murmuring into her hair. "I'm okay with that."

They lay that way for a while, silent, holding each other in the aftermath of truth. It was jarring and simplistic, that truth. For the first time in years, they weren't hiding anything from each other or dancing around what their relationship was or wasn't, but accepting it as is. She loved him, plain and simple, and it was terrifying and exhilarating and precarious. Like she was tumbling through the sky, no longer certain which way was up.

"I dream."

Tyler's voice broke the silence, a bare murmur into her hair. His heart beneath her ear hammered. When he began to tremble as well, instinct told her his mind had traveled into the past. She lifted her head, peering at the dark shape of his face. He was little more than a shadow against the darkness pervading the room, but somberness had risen over him.

She reached up, stroking his cheek. "About what happened?"

"Mmm. Lately, I dream about you." He paused and a shiver ran through him. When he spoke again, his voice came low and filled with pain. "You're screaming, and I can't get to you."

The image filled her mind, what he must have seen, what he relived every night, and her heart clenched, tears flooding her eyes. She hated the thought of the things they'd done to him. It became a physical pain, aching in her chest to the point she feared it would crack open. She'd give anything to take his agony from him.

She kissed his chest again, over his heart, and wrapped her arm around his waist, hugging him as tightly as she could, given their position. "I'm safe, Ty, and so are you."

"It doesn't feel like it. That's the ugly part I hate telling you about. I'm thirty years old, and I'm terrified of the damn dark. I have to sleep with a light on and the bedroom door open. If Mom closes it, I usually wake in a panic. Just riding the elevator up to your castle in the sky makes me break out in a cold sweat." He let out a heavy sigh, his voice becoming a murmur between them. "It's also the real reason we didn't go to a movie tonight. I'm not sure I could handle sitting in a cramped, dark room."

Catching the significance of his words, she lifted her head. "Would you prefer I turn the light on?"

He let out a harsh laugh. "No. Makes me feel like a damn child. The dream is an ugly twist on something that happened. One of the soldiers captured was a woman. They…" He stopped, audibly swallowing. "I think they raped her. They kept us separate from each other, but close enough that I could hear them."

The image bombarded her mind, what it must have been like for him, sitting in a dark cell, hearing those awful sounds. She couldn't stop the shudder from moving through her, something he must have caught because he buried his face in her hair, his voice a shaky whisper against her cheek.

"What I remember most, what sticks with me, is her screaming. She was one of the last to die. I tried to get to her. Pretty sure I threw my shoulder out hurling myself against that goddamn door, but it wouldn't budge, and I ended up sitting on the dirt floor crying along with her."

She swallowed past the lump in her throat but couldn't stop the tears from escaping. It was too much to imagine, the horror he went through, the terror and desperation. "Is that why you dream of me?"

"In the dream, I'm locked in the same room, but you're the one screaming. God, the pain in your voice, your sobbing…" He drew a breath that vibrated through him, and several seconds passed in strained silence before he spoke again. "But I can't get to you. I can't get out the fucking door. I can't save you. In the end, I heard them all die."

The pain in his voice cracked the wall in her chest. The tears overflowed, unstoppable. For the horror he'd endured, for the people he'd lost and the burden their losses had left on him. She buried her face in his chest, hugging him hard, and prayed he couldn't feel her tears, because she couldn't stop them. When his arms banded around her in turn, crushing her to him, a sob escaped her, and she lifted her face, finding his mouth in the darkness. He kissed her hard, his body shaking against her, salt on his tongue as it pushed into her mouth, restless and searching. Reaching up to stroke his cheek, her fingers found wetness.

Knowing he trusted her enough to not only stay the night but also to share the horrors he'd experienced, to share his nightmares and allow himself to cry in front of her awed and amazed her. She yearned to tell him everything trapped in her chest. That she was damn lucky to get him back. That she wasn't ever letting him go. All she could do was cling to his shoulders and kiss him back, pouring the words she couldn't find into the intense connection.

When they broke apart, they were both breathing hard. Tyler rested his forehead against hers, his cock stiff against the softness of her belly. She moved away enough to reach into the nightstand drawer, pulled out another condom, and handed it to him. The sound of foil ripping filled the silence as he tore open the packet. After putting on the condom, he reached down and hooked her knee, pulling it over his hip, then slid his hand to her ass and held her in place as he plunged deep.

He wasn't slow or soft this time. Instead, their lovemaking took on a desperate edge. He used his purchase to pull her into him, his every thrust a powerful surge. Cassie dug her nails into his shoulders and thrust hard against him in return, reaching for something she couldn't name but that gripped her chest all the same. The need to be as close as possible. To climb inside him and never come back out. The fear still gripped her chest. That he'd evaporate into the ether and she'd lose him again. Or wake up to find out this last week had only been a beautiful dream.

The sounds filled the room around her, a cacophony of their desperation for each other. The slap of flesh on flesh. His grunts. Her soft moans. They ignited a fire in each other. Every little sound she made, he groaned and pushed in deeper. Each hard thrust set a blaze burning through her blood and sent her hurtling toward climax at a speed that left her breathless and gasping.

It didn't last long. In a few dozen strokes, they were shuddering together, his quiet groan mixing with the choked cries she failed to contain.

When it was over, they lay silent, still joined. Cassie trembled as she listened to Tyler's harsh breathing and the wild thumping of his heartbeat at the base of his throat. The last wall between them had shattered to dust. Their lovemaking had often been intense. Tyler took her to places no other man ever had, before or since.

This experience had leveled her. She was sure she'd given her soul to him and taken his in return and an ultravulnerable sensation caught in her chest.

The thought left her somewhere between the delirious need to laugh like a lunatic and being too stunned to do much more than hold on to him. She feared if she let him go, she'd come apart at the seams. Three years ago—hell even six months ago—she'd have said she didn't believe in that kind of "nonsense," that it wasn't possible to give someone your soul. Right then, taking each breath with him, she knew she had.

Still breathing hard, he dropped his forehead onto her shoulder with a heavy sigh. "I'm sorry. I just…I needed you."

"Don't be sorry. I needed you, too." She turned her head, kissing his neck, his jaw, his chin, any part of him she could reach. It was the most vulnerable she'd ever been and the most free, and it filled her with questions she didn't know how to answer. What happened now?

And yet even as she asked herself the question, several more popped up right behind it. How could she ever let him go? How could she ever have been delusional enough to think that she could?

* * *

They had her again. From somewhere in the distance, Williams's screams pierced the awful silence of the night. The agony in her voice shredded his insides and ripped his chest open.

Sore. He was so fucking sore. Every limb ached. His shoulder hurt like hell. Throwing himself against that door hadn't done a damn thing except probably dislocate his shoulder.

"I'm here."

The soft voice sounded through the darkness, faint, like the whispers of a ghost. He jerked his head up, searching the darkness.

Cassie.

The screams shifted, Williams's voice rising in pitch, mixing with Cassie's. Until they rang in his head, piercing his eardrums.

"Ty, I'm here…"

The voice sounded again, followed by more screaming. So much agony and fear. It gnawed at his insides like crows pecking at a carcass. He was useless. Fucking useless. They were over there doing God knew what to her, and he was here, sitting in the dark, crying like a five-year-old.

Because he couldn't help her. He couldn't get to her.

He couldn't even help himself.

Her screams ceased, cut off abruptly. Panic curled through him. Her screams always dwindled before they stopped. He'd hear her whimpering. Now only aching, deafening silence enveloped him. Heart hammering in his throat, he turned his head, listening, praying, but long minutes passed in awful silence. Deep down, in a place he couldn't explain even to himself, he knew she wouldn't answer. Ever again.

A hand slid over his shoulder, the fingers warm and soft. Startled, Tyler swore and rolled, scrambling to get away. Where had they come from? He hadn't heard the heavy door open. Its rusty hinges groaned. How the hell had they gotten in without him hearing?

In his haste, he fell over some sort of ledge, his hand

catching the edge of a solid object, sending it crashing to the floor with him, where he landed hard on his ass. He turned his head, scanning the darkness for the threat, when a shadow caught his attention. It moved in his direction, a black arm reaching for him, fingers stretching.

"It's okay, Ty. I'm okay. You're okay."

Cassie. Her words were soft, but their meaning rushed over him, and grief hit his gut with the force of a meaty fist. No. He wasn't okay. He'd never be okay again. They'd taken her from him. What the hell did he have to live for now? They'd taken them all, one by one, then took her, too.

The shadow moved again, thin fingers reaching through the darkness like the hand of death. He ducked and rolled, determined to get out of reach. If they were taking him now, he'd go down fighting.

Before he could draw his next breath, he was scrambling to his feet. Something sharp sliced into his instep, and he swore under his breath, favoring his injured foot.

"Tyler, don't move!"

Feet thumped the floor and a click sounded, the room flooding with light. The sudden brightness froze him in his spot, momentarily disorienting him. As his eyes adjusted, he turned his head, scanning the room around him, and found…nothing he'd expected. He faced a familiar baby blue wall as he stood beside a white nightstand he'd seen more than a dozen times. Confused, he turned the other direction. Glass crunched beneath his feet, jagged pieces cutting into the sole of his foot, but the pain didn't register.

"Ty, don't move. You knocked over the lamp."

Cassie's voice wafted over him. She rounded the end of the bed, her face twisted in concern. She was naked and the back of her hair was mussed, locks of it sticking up at odd angles, but she looked like an angel. So damn beautiful that for a moment, he could only stare. Was she real? Or was this another dream?

He reached out to her and turned, needing to touch her, to know, when she gripped his arm hard, stopping his movement.

She nodded at the floor. "Glass, honey. You broke the lamp."

And that's when the dream snapped shut and reality slammed him against the wall. He was in Cassie's penthouse. In her room.

She looked down, the grooves between her brows deepening. "You cut your foot. Sit, Ty. I need to clean up the glass; then I'll help you with your foot, okay?"

Cassie didn't wait for an answer but turned and ran from the bedroom, her rapid footsteps echoing down the hall. It wasn't until he followed her gaze, looking down at the floor, that it hit him what had happened. Splotches of red blood now stained her white carpeting.

"Fuck." He dropped onto the end of the bed and rested his elbows on his knees, ducking his head into his hands. The dreams. He must have called out in his sleep. She must have reached for him, and he'd reacted.

Before he could think much more than that, Cassie rushed back into the room, a brown paper bag in one hand and a small vacuum in the other. She set the vacuum aside and squatted in front of him, glancing at him as she picked up the big pieces of her broken lamp and tossed them into the bag. "I want to clean up the glass first. Then I'll take a look at your foot."

Forget that. "Are you okay?" His voice came out hoarse. Had he been screaming? Or just talking? His mother told him he often did both. Shame rose to suffocate him. He hated knowing Cassie had been privy to that.

"I'm fine. You were calling my name in your sleep." She dropped another chunk of what looked to be an expensive lamp into the bag and offered a wobbly smile.

He didn't miss the way her fingers trembled or that while her smile was pleasant, the sentiment didn't reach her eyes.

"I didn't hurt you?" He held his breath, waiting, scanning her body for any sign he might have struck out at her before realizing she wasn't one of the insurgents who'd captured him. No red welts or fingerprints. Her skin was still as perfect as ever.

She froze, her head jerking in his direction, eyes going wide and round. The same look he remembered that night three years ago, when he'd sank to his knees and asked her to marry him. Just this side of panicked. Her chest rose and fell at a rapid pace as well, and she swallowed before blinking and shaking her head. She dropped the bag and pushed to her feet, maneuvered the glass on the carpet, and sank to the bed beside him.

She reached out, her fingers trembling in the air for a moment before settling over his knee. "You would never hurt me, Ty."

His gaze had stuck on her trembling fingers, his senses honing in on her soft body against his side. "Then why are you shaking?"

She laughed, light and airy, the sound someone makes in a hysterical moment. "'Cause you scared the hell out of me. I wasn't prepared for you to go launching out of bed."

The weight of her revelation and what it meant—that she'd been privy to his humiliation—pressed down on him, and his shoulders slumped. He was a fucking mess. They were just getting back on track, but what good did it do him? He couldn't give her what she wanted. She needed him to stay, to hold her while she slept, and he couldn't. He wasn't even sure it was safe anymore.

Never mind that he couldn't take care of her. He didn't have a job. He had a vague prospect, one that required he be mentally competent. Yeah, he was pretty sure he was failing *that* particular test. He was fucking useless.

"I'm sorry. I should go. I'm not sure this was a good idea." Numb now and too damn tired, he pushed to his feet, ignoring the pain shooting through his sole as he scanned the room for his clothing.

Cassie surged to her feet and moved in front of him, blocking his path. All five feet six inches of her. Her eyes narrowed as she braced a hand against his chest and jabbed a finger at the bed behind him. "No you don't. Sit. Down."

Helplessness washed over him. All he could see was the room. The shattered lamp. The splotches of blood staining her carpet. The chaos he'd brought to her quiet life.

He swept his hand in the air. "Look at your room, Cass.

This is life with me now. This isn't a once in a while thing. This is an everyday occurrence for me. If you want to sleep with me, you can't ever close the bedroom door. More often than not, I sleep with the TV on, because it acts like a night-light. Hell, I've flat-out asked Mom to turn the light on a few times, because it felt safer than sleeping in the fucking dark. I have no idea when I'll be able to go back into one of those clubs you love so much. Or a movie theater. Or hell, a crowded restaurant."

He was breathing hard by the time he finished. There it was. His entire pathetic self wrapped up in a neat little bow. Yeah, some boyfriend he was. And he wanted to marry her? Have kids he could hurt as easily? To ask her to settle for a life filled with this crap? God, she deserved so much better than this. So much better than him.

Cassie froze again, staring at him. Tense seconds passed as those eyes searched his. He wasn't sure he wanted to know what she thought, wasn't sure he could handle it, but the longer he watched, the more her beautiful eyes filled with tears. They hovered at the edges of her lashes, stubborn, like her. Finally, she swallowed, blinked, and her shoulders rounded. "And you somehow think that changes how I feel?"

It should. He wouldn't blame her if it did. A relationship with him wasn't easy or uncomplicated anymore. He came with baggage. Big, heavy fucking luggage he didn't know if *he* could carry anymore. Why the hell should he expect her to?

"Doesn't it?" He dragged a hand over his head, clutching

the short hairs on top. Instinct told him to look away, to hide from her, but he couldn't stop watching her eyes. He needed her response like he needed to breathe or eat.

A single tear escaped, trailing down her cheek, but she swiped it away and drew her shoulders back.

"No. Now sit down, damn it. I need to clean this up first, so neither of us gets cuts again, and then I'm going to take care of your foot. If we don't get that glass out, it'll get infected. We can talk when I'm done." She planted her hands on her hips and stood glaring at him like a fucking drill sergeant. When he didn't move—because he was too awed by her to do much more than stare—she jabbed her finger in the direction of the bed again. "Sit."

So he sat, because who the hell could argue with her?

Chapter Twelve

Cassie bent to the mess spread out around her, picking up as much of the broken glass as possible and chucking it into the bag. Tyler sat on the bed. He was quiet, too much so, and he wouldn't look at her. Rather, his shoulders rounded, elbows resting on his knees, and his head sat in his hands. She couldn't even tell if he breathed.

The moment of truth had arrived. She had a decision to make, a big one, and she was pretty sure she knew the answer. They needed each other. What she had to do now was be honest with him. So she started talking, because she didn't know what else *to* do.

"You know, when I met you, all I wanted was a fling. Since Nick's death, I lived by certain rules. I didn't date men in uniform, and I didn't allow myself to get close to anyone, because I couldn't handle losing someone else. But God you were gorgeous in that uniform, with your bulging muscles and throwing those one-liners at me with that cocky damn grin on your face."

Remembering made her shiver again. Running headlong into a pair of strong arms, only to find him grinning at her. And then he'd tossed that awful line at her. She was pretty sure she'd fallen for him that night.

She shook her head, picked up another large shard of glass, and tossed it into the paper bag. She could only pray she was reaching him. "I'd convinced myself you were just a fling, that I wasn't falling for you, but when I was with you, I felt good. Free. You were the one man in my life who didn't seem to want anything from me. You accepted me as I was, crabby and demanding and all. Hell, you laughed at me for it, teased me.

"Nobody's ever done that for me. Even my father wants me to be something I'm not. But when you dropped to your knees and asked me to marry you, it scared the hell out of me. You were leaving and it meant I could lose you. Like my mother. Like Nick. When you didn't come home…"

Her voice cracked, and she stopped to collect herself as the memories of that time, when Marilyn had called to tell her the news, filled her mind. The pain that had wrenched at her chest. The months of trying but failing to go numb. To somehow figure out how she'd live without him. The shame of realizing she'd fallen in love with a man who'd died thinking he meant so little to her.

She drew a shuddering breath. She was telling him all of this, because she wanted, *needed*, him to know. She had the distinct feeling he was making decisions, ones that didn't include *her*.

Out of the corner of her eye, she saw Tyler lift his head but he remained silent, watching her, somberness emanating from him.

She swiped at the tears, picked up another chunk of her broken lamp, and went on. If she was losing him, fine, but she'd do everything not to. He'd at least know what he really meant to her.

"Somewhere along the way I fell in love with you. You want to know what I did when I thought you died? I buried the pain. In alcohol. In other men. I pushed myself to the limits, because it was easier than admitting I couldn't live without you. My life doesn't make sense without you, Ty. So all this crap?"

She swiped her hand in the air, encompassing the mess around her.

"This is just stuff. I can buy a new lamp. What I need is *you*. In any way you'll let me. If that means you have to go home at the end of the night, fine. Do what you have to do, but don't think for one second that I care about this mess or how fucked up you are. Because you're alive, Tyler. *Alive.*"

Tyler remained silent. Tension rose in the room like a dense fog, until she was sure something would break between them. He'd shut himself off from her. Never in all the time she'd known him had he ever gone to a place she couldn't reach. Was this what he felt like all those times she'd shut *him* out? Her cheeks heated, shame rising over her. How could she ever have treated him like he was nothing? Tyler was her everything. The sun her world revolved around.

Unable to stand his silence, she chucked another piece of her broken lamp into the bag with a little more force than necessary and jerked her gaze to him. "Say something, damn it."

He'd been staring at the floor but lifted his gaze. Those blue eyes she loved so much, normally bright and playful, were now devoid of emotion, blank and unreachable. "What do you want me to say?"

Heart aching, she abandoned the mess and maneuvered around it, coming to squat at his feet. "Talk to me. I know I deserve the silent treatment, because I've done the same to you too many times, but please don't shut me out."

He ducked his head, running trembling hands back and forth over the top. "I don't know if I can do this, Cass. I'm barely making it through the day. I can't ask you to live with this."

She reached out carefully, allowing him time to adjust to her movements, and rested her hands on his knees. Somehow, she hoped the touch would ground them together. It always had in the past. "What, you mean like the way I've asked you to live with my moodiness? To deal with my need to be perfect all the time?"

His head snapped up then, and the hurt in those beautiful blue eyes took her breath away. His walls were crumbling. "This goes a little beyond you being moody, don't you think? It's like living with a fucking child. I can't ask you to do that. Never mind that I could have hurt you. It happens, you know. Guys who end up beating the hell out of their wives because they're lost in a flashback and don't realize it until it's too late. I thought you were one of them. When I came to and you reached for me in the dark? I thought you were one of *them*."

His voice cracked, and he ducked his head, drawing a deep breath that vibrated through him.

"I beat the hell out of one of them once. I was winning, too. Right before I got the butt end of a rifle to the back of my head. I woke up chained to a fucking cement wall with the mother of all headaches."

Her heart twisted. He truly believed what he said, that he was a walking time bomb, ready to detonate at any second. She ached to wrap her arms around him and hold him until he stopped shaking, but would he even let her? She settled, instead, for taking his hands and peering into his face. "You would never hurt me, Ty."

She knew that with every fiber of her being. Whoever he fought in his dreams, given what he'd told her, he appeared to be trying to save someone. That was Tyler in a nutshell. The big guy with a heart of gold.

He laughed, bitter and sardonic. "I'm glad *you* think so, because I'm not so sure anymore."

"I *am* sure. I spooked you. That's all it was. I have some adjusting to do. We'll have to learn how to be together again. I have a few repeat customers who have sons with PTSD. I can ask for advice. What I can't do is live without you. Been there, tried that. It didn't work."

He gave a slow, miserable shake of his head. His voice

lowered to a pained murmur, so quiet she had to lean in to hear him. "I can't even take care of you, Cass. I'm an emotional wreck. I don't have a job. Just the vague prospect of one. One I likely won't get because I'm no doubt going to fail those psych evals. I'd be asking you to accept half the man you deserve."

She reached up, meaning to stroke his cheek, but he flinched, and she sighed, pulling her hand back. "You went through something, Ty. You have to give yourself time to heal from it. And no offense, baby, but I don't *need* you to take care of me. I just need you to make love to me, then hold me while I sleep."

Tossing humor at him was a desperate attempt to reach him, but it worked. His hard façade cracked, one corner of his mouth hitching upward. "Leave it to you to bring sex into this."

She let out a quiet laugh and ducked her head to look him in the eye again. "I need you, Ty. I need you in my life. If you can handle my fucked-up-ness, I can handle yours."

He looked up then, meeting her gaze. His had softened around the edges, his eyes still tormented but more open than they'd been. He lifted a hand, caressing her cheek with his fingers, awe in his voice. "I love you, you know that? I don't deserve you, but I do love you."

"And I *know* I don't deserve you. I'm pretty sure you should have left my ass a long time ago, but I'm afraid you're stuck with me." She glanced down at the blood-stained carpeting and smiled. "Now how 'bout we get you cleaned up, hmm? You're bleeding on my carpet."

* * *

Two weeks later…

Cassie came awake to quiet moaning and someone calling her name. Disoriented, she opened her eyes, blinking at the dark ceiling above her, and listened for whatever had woken her. Beside her, Tyler shifted on the bed, letting out a quiet moan.

"No. Cassie!"

She turned onto her side, facing him. He lay on his side as well, features twisted in agony. For a moment, she could only watch him, heart heavy. Every night for the last fourteen days, it had been the same. He stayed—because she'd asked him to—and every night, he had the dreams. Nights were torture for him. He was always restless beside her, moaning or calling out someone's name. Sometimes the name of the woman captured with him, sometimes Cassie's, but every time his voice filled with anguish.

It hurt her heart to watch him struggle with himself. He had to watch his friends die, had had to listen to his attackers rape and torture them, had been tortured himself. It had all etched itself on his soul. She couldn't help wondering if her presence brought this out in him. Were the dreams worse because he slept beside *her*? Or were they always this bad?

He called out again, this time reaching toward her. Cassie clutched his fingers, giving them a reassuring squeeze. Instead of him quieting and settling back to sleep, though, his eyes snapped open, searching her face in wide-eyed panic.

"It's okay, Ty. It's just me. I'm here."

He didn't seem to hear her. Rather, his eyes widened further, and before she could blink, he sprang into motion, rolling over the top of her. He leaned his upper body into her, holding her down with his chest and shoulders, then used his hands to pull her wrists to her sides and set his knees on her arms. Before she could even think of what to do, he'd effectively rendered her helpless.

Her pulse kicked up several notches, thundering in her ears, as panic rose over her. Shit. What the hell did she do now?

He laid one hand across her throat, a casual threat, and leaned down, until she was taking each breath with him. "I'm going to take your fucking head off."

The deathly calm in his voice had fear slithering like ice down her spine as the realization sank over her at what, exactly, was happening. He was lost in his dream. Night terrors. Isn't that what they called this? Or was this a flashback? Jesus. She didn't know, but the beautiful blue eyes she'd stared into a thousand times didn't seem to see *her* at all. They were unfocused, flitting back and forth, filled with a mix of emotion that made her want to weep. Pain. Anger.

Fear.

"For every time you raped her. For every injury you caused them. For every day you shoved that rifle in my face, for every beating, and for every single fucking one of their deaths."

He leaned into her, pressing his nose to hers, his hot, harsh breaths puffing against her mouth. Hot tears burned behind Cassie's eyelids. She'd have to wake him up. Her chest clenched and her eyes refilled. When he came around, he'd no doubt hate himself, but if she didn't stop him…

She swallowed past the lump burning in her throat and drew her wits about her. "Tyler, wake up. Come on, soldier boy, wake up."

When he didn't move or even acknowledge that he'd heard her, she pushed against his hold on her arms, attempting to touch him, but to no avail. He outweighed her by fifty pounds at least. She could barely flap her hands, let alone lift them. Hot tears rolled from the corners of her eyes as her mind took the moment and ran. Was this how he'd felt? Trapped and helpless?

"I'm going to make sure you can't hurt anyone ever again."

He leaned on her throat this time, making it harder to breathe. Wetness dropped onto her cheek, Tyler's tears mixing with hers. He was crying, mourning in his sleep for the friends he'd lost, for the pain he'd endured. Cassie bit back a choked sob and her chest tightened until she couldn't breathe. Even angry, his only thought wasn't revenge, but fighting to save his friends. For the woman whose terror-filled screams he relived night after night.

She swallowed hard, drew a shaky breath, and tried again. Stretching her fingers as far as she could, she managed to stroke his thigh and tried to keep her voice as calm as possible. "It's Cassie. Wake up, Tyler. You're safe. Do you hear me? You're safe. You're with me. It's over."

By the time she finished, her voice was wobbling with the pain and fear she couldn't hold back. She should have done her research. She should have insisted they talk about this. It hadn't sunk in exactly how bad it was for him, had stupidly thought she could handle whatever he went through on her own. As it was, she had no idea how to reach him.

Tyler froze above her, stared at her for a second, and cocked his head to the side. "Cassie?"

She stretched her fingers out again, caressing his thigh with the tips. "That's right, it's me. You're dreaming. Turn on the light, honey. Get up and turn on the light. It's just a dream."

He tilted his head to look between their bodies. Moving slowly, he released her and sat upright, straddling her stomach. She couldn't see his eyes anymore, but his questioning gaze burned into her. Without a word, he climbed off her and made his way to the switch on the wall beside the door. When the light flicked on, illuminating the darkness, Tyler turned, blinking against the sudden brightness. He stared at her, gaze searching, brow twisted in confusion.

Cassie sat up, leaned back against the headboard, and massaged the feeling back into her hands. Heart thumping, she let him have the moment to himself. She didn't want to startle him any more than she already had.

Finally, he blinked, and understanding and recognition dawned over him. Regret took shape in his eyes, and he drew his shoulders back, standing straight and stiff. "What did I do?"

The barely contained panic in his voice had a lump rising in her throat. Unable to bear watching his reaction, she shut her eyes.

"Please don't ask." She plastered on the best smile she could muster. "Just come back to bed. Leave the light on and come back to bed."

"What did I do, Cassie?"

This time, his tone was a command and a plea. A single tear rolled from the corner of her eye. She couldn't tell him this. It would be a wound on his soul. He'd think himself a monster, and she couldn't do that to him.

"God, I hurt you, didn't I?"

His words drifted to her, small and quiet but full of an acceptance that made her stomach hurt. She opened her eyes but wished she hadn't. The anguish in his beautiful blues was too much to bear. He'd already accepted his statement as fact.

She shook her head. "You didn't hurt me, I promise. You just…pinned me to the bed."

She didn't have the courage to tell him what he'd said to her. It was more than enough to know he'd touched her in anger at all. No way could she tell him he'd threatened her. He wouldn't care that technically he'd threatened the person he thought her to be.

Tyler strode around the end of the bed, stood over her, brow furrowed in determination, and held out his hands. "Let me see."

"Don't do this, Ty. Nothing good will come of it." She patted the bed beside her. "Just come back to bed."

He shook his hands, the grooves between his brows deepening. "Let. Me. See."

She closed her eyes, unable to stop a couple more tears

from rolling down her cheeks. When she didn't obey his demand, Tyler picked up her wrists, turning them over. Several seconds passed in silence. Tension rose over the room. Cassie's heart clenched.

"Jesus Christ."

He released her arms, and Cassie opened her eyes. Tyler stood by the side of the bed, dragging his hands over the top of his head, eyes wide as saucers. She scooted across the bed and reached out, but before she could make contact, Tyler backed away from her. "I need to go home. This was such a bad idea."

"Please don't go."

If he heard her, he didn't acknowledge her, but he made his way around the room, gathering his clothing from where he'd flung it the night before and got dressed. He pulled on and buttoned his jeans, yanked on his T-shirt, shoved his feet into his socks, and headed for the bedroom door without so much as a backward glance.

The aching in her heart told her she was losing him. Even that awful night three years ago, when they'd hurled insults at each other and he'd told her to get the hell out of his apartment, he'd never shut her out. Tyler always had something to say. Now he simply turned and left, back stiff, shoulders straight. A man who keeps moving because he has to.

When he reached the door, panic closed around her, and she called out to him, desperate to stop him.

"Will I see you later?" God, she was the needy girl all over again, but she couldn't think of anything else to say that might stop him.

"I don't know." Tyler didn't so much as glance in her direction but moved through the doorway, striding away from her like a man on a mission. Seconds later, the front door closed with a quiet snap, leaving her alone in the aching silence.

Cassie scooted to the end of the bed, staring at the empty doorway. One by one, tears collected in her eyes. She was losing him all over again.

Chapter Thirteen

Tyler stared at his phone, seated on the table in front of him. His breakfast went forgotten as he pulled up Cassie's number and her face flashed on the small screen. God, how he ached to call her. Just to hear her voice. A week had passed since he'd seen her, and he was definitely going through withdrawals. He missed every damn thing about her. Her smile. Her laugh. The stubborn lift of her chin when she was determined to do something.

He'd done a lot of thinking over the last week. That night in her condo had been a low point. It made him take a good long look at his life and what he wanted from it, and he only knew one thing: he wanted her. If he ever hoped to get back, he had to stop sitting around feeling sorry for himself and start learning how to live like a normal person again. And it started by admitting he couldn't do it on his own. That he needed help.

Cassie had ended up being his inspiration. His reason to

pick himself up and get moving. The same way she had while he was in Iraq. Sitting in that dank cell, she'd been his reason to keep fighting. She'd saved him.

He hated himself for the way he'd treated her this week. He hadn't so much as called her, and she had to be feeling like he'd tossed her aside, like she meant nothing to him. At first, he was simply overwhelmed by it all. The fear of hurting her lived and breathed inside of him, no longer a simple worry, but a distinct possibility. But before he could ever trust himself around her again, he wanted a working plan of action.

Now he just had to pray it worked. Because he couldn't lose her. Not again.

His mother glanced at him as she came around the corner. Dressed and ready for work, she called to him as she made her way into the kitchen. "I'm almost ready. Just let me grab some coffee, then we can go."

He shook his head, raising his voice so she could hear him in the kitchen as he closed the screen on his phone. "Do you really think she'll go for it?"

Thanks to the new therapist he was seeing, he now had a plan, one he was about to set into motion. The question was, would Cassie even want to see him? When she figured out she wasn't meeting his mother, would she turn around and walk away? That was the thing, he couldn't be sure he'd blame her if she did. He only knew he had to try. For her.

He rested his elbow on the table and raked a hand through his hair. His military crew cut had grown out over the last month. Now when he dragged his fingers through it, he couldn't stop seeing Cassie's long nails doing the same thing. The way her small, slender fingers would slide along his scalp. God, that was bliss.

"I can't stop seeing the look on her face. She's never looked at me like that before." The fear in Cassie's eyes that night haunted him. She'd tried to hide it, but he'd seen it. He'd scared the hell out of her. "I left marks on her wrists. I could have done real damage. She managed to reach me before my mind got too far into the memory, but what if she can't next time?"

His mother came out of the kitchen, coffee cup in one hand, and laid the other on his shoulder. "You went through something traumatic, and you're healing. That makes you human, not a monster. You're not alone anymore. It's time to let her back in. Let her help you find the answers." She bent to kiss the top of his head. "I'm ready. Drop me at work, then take my car and go get your girl."

* * *

By the time he made it to the fountain at the base of the Space Needle, he was fifteen minutes late. His mother had told Cassie to meet her here at one, but traffic getting down here had been a bitch. Paper shopping bag tucked under one arm, he jogged down the sidewalk from the parking lot, scanning the area as he ran. It was a rare sunny day. The clouds had cleared, which meant everyone had come outside to enjoy it. People littered the area, but Cassie was nowhere to be seen.

Doubt rose over him. Maybe she'd figured it all out and had decided not to come. Or maybe she'd gotten tired of waiting and went home.

He was late because he'd stopped at a repair shop on his way there. He'd decided something else this week. He was leaving the army behind. The realization had come to him while he worked on his bike late one night. He had no desire to go back overseas and relive the hell. Doing so would likely only make everything worse, which would do nothing but set him back to square one. He wanted to move forward, not backward.

So he'd called his commanding officer after talking to his mother this morning. He'd given Intel the info he knew on the insurgents who'd held him, for the families of the soldiers who died, but he was getting on with his life. And it started with getting a job.

The idea had come to him after a phone call he'd gotten yesterday. One of the guys he'd served with had seen him on the news and looked him up. Turned out, he owned a custom bike shop. So he'd gone down there on a wing and a prayer. What started out as a conversation between friends ended with them offering him a job.

For the first time since he'd gotten home, outside of the time he spent with Cassie, he didn't feel so damn useless. Having somewhere to go every day and friends to hang out with who understood his struggles went a long way toward helping him feel human again. It was one more item that would hopefully prove to her that he could be what she needed.

Tyler came to a stop at the edge of the grassy expanse surrounding the Space Needle and turned, scanning the area again when a sight halted him in his tracks. Cassie. She strode across the grass, her head turning as if in search of something. Or some*one*.

The simple sight of her threatened to bring him to his knees. A week felt like forever. To see her here, of all places, filled him with hope. This was where they'd met. Four years ago, at the Fourth of July fireworks display they threw every year at the Needle. She'd barreled into him at the edge of the grass right over there. Instead of a short skirt, though, she wore jeans, and those blasted black boots instead of heels, but she looked just as gorgeous.

Finally, her gaze landed on him, and she stopped. Tyler held his breath and waited.

"What are you doing here?" She darted a glance around, confusion written in the lines of her forehead. "I was expecting to meet your mother."

"I know. And I'm sorry for the deception, but I wasn't sure you'd come if you knew it was me." He tucked his free hand in his pocket and readjusted the bag he held under his right arm. "I have something to share with you. I asked Mom to get you downtown, because I wanted to say it in a place that holds good memories for us."

She folded her arms and looked off to her left. Despite the stiffness of her stance, something vulnerable hung on her. "It's been a week, Tyler. You haven't so much as called me. You could've let me know you were okay, you know."

Guilt caged his chest. She was right. "I know. At first, I

was just lost and overwhelmed. I didn't trust myself with you. I could've really hurt you, Cass. I don't think I could live with myself if I ever did."

"And now?" She turned her head, hope infusing her searching gaze, filling him with the same emotion.

He pulled the bag out from under his arm, holding it up to show her. "Now I'm a bit better armed. I've started seeing a therapist and we've been going through ways he thinks could help me get a handle on this. I have so much I want to tell you, to show you. I just need five minutes."

She stared for so long he was sure she'd turn him down, but she drew a breath, her shoulders slumping as she blew it out. "Okay."

Joy exploded through him, expanding in his chest like the sun blooming inside of him. Feeling too much like a little kid hopped up on too much sugar and let loose in a toy store, he could barely contain himself. It was all he could do to simply stand there. He wanted to shout. To pick her up and twirl her around. Christ. He hadn't expected her to say that.

"Thank you." He gripped the shopping bag in trembling hands, swallowed down the icy fear rising over him, and stepped toward her. Now came the moment of truth. "But I need to ask you something first, and I need you to be honest with me."

She stared for a moment, gaze reaching and searching, before finally nodding. "What?"

He took another step toward her, hovering over her now. The soft scent of her perfume blew in on a soft breeze, curling around his senses like a lure. It was the most vulnerable damn thing he'd ever asked her. "Do you still love me?"

Shock moved over her features. Her eyes widened. Her jaw dropped open. Tears slowly gathered in the corners of her eyes. "How could you even ask me that?"

The quiet disbelief and hurt that laced her tone cut into him like a knife with a jagged blade, but that she'd asked him had to be good.

"I just need to need to hear you say it. I walked out on you, Cassie, not knowing if I'd ever see you again. I didn't trust myself. If I ever hurt you..." Fear rose over him like a suffocating shroud, but he swallowed it down. Forced himself to focus on the moment. On her. "My point is, I wouldn't exactly blame you if you decided you were done with me. But I have to admit I'm kind of hoping you aren't."

Cassie, stubborn, willful woman that she was, squared her shoulders and hiked her chin a notch. "You know damn well I love you."

For a moment, he couldn't breathe, could only stand there and stare at the vision she made. Those words from her sweet mouth were like feeling the sun on his face for the first time after months of being kept in the dark. They illuminated the dark places inside of him.

"Thank you. I just needed to hear you say it." He wanted to cup her face in his hands, plaster his mouth on hers, and kiss the hell out of her. As it was, he needed to take this slowly, one step at a time. So he glanced down at the bag in his hands, opened the top, and held it out to her. "I bought something. Mostly for me, but really, well, for us."

She glanced at the bag but didn't take it. "What is it?"

Hands shaking, Tyler reached inside and pulled out the small box, then slung the bag's handles over his forearm. "It's a heart rate monitor. Most people use it for training, but it has an alarm that goes off when you go above your target heart rate."

She shook her head. "I'm not following you. What's this have to do with us?"

He pulled the small, black plastic wristband out of the box and held it up to show her. It was a cross between a bracelet and a stopwatch. "I spoke to a therapist and more than a dozen ex-military who all have the same problems I do. PTSD with night terrors. A lot of them told me they use something like this to help them get through the night."

She took the device and turned it over in her hands, darting a glance at him as she examined it. "And you think this could help us?"

"When my heart rate starts to go up, when the dreams start, the alarm will go off. I'm told if it doesn't wake me up outright, it should, at least, shift the dreams and calm me down. A lot of the men I spoke with said it helped stop the nightmares and that they slept better. I'll need time to test it out, though. Three nights. If it helps, have dinner with me. Your place, Friday night, six o'clock. I'll cook. Or maybe we can order in. Hell. I don't know. I wanted to tell you first."

She opened her mouth, but he put his finger to her lips, halting the words before they left her mouth.

"I love you, Cassie. I scared the hell out of myself last week. I'll admit it. But I'm not giving up. I have more I want to tell you, but this is the most important. I need to know this works before I'll really be able to trust myself. What do you say, sweetheart? Three more days, then dinner on Friday?"

She closed her mouth, stared for so long he was sure she'd turn him down, then finally nodded. "Okay. Dinner on Friday."

Unable to resist touching her any longer, he cupped her face in his palms and kissed her softly. "Thank you. For having faith in me. I won't be late. I promise."

* * *

Five minutes past six on Friday evening, the hope Cassie had built for three days sank into her toes. Standing in the center of her immaculate kitchen, staring at the Styrofoam containers on the counter, her heart thumped a dull, painful beat. It was only five minutes, but it had her mind spinning into awful places. Maybe the heart monitor hadn't worked.

The last three days had driven her crazy. Too many hours spent lying in her bed, waiting, worrying. If this didn't work...

The doorbell sounded through the condo, and Cassie jerked her gaze in the direction of the entry hallway; then she ran for the front door, flinging it open in abandon.

Tyler stood in the vestibule, thumbs casually hooked in his pockets, and for a moment, she soaked in the sight of him. He looked good. Not as tired. His eyes were bright, the smile he gave her soft. "Hey."

What she wanted to do was to fling herself at him. This

was a good sign. This was a *damn* good sign. That he'd come had to mean the heart monitor had worked. Didn't it?

She fisted her hands but couldn't contain the giddy hopefulness blossoming in her chest. "Does this mean what I think it does?"

He hitched a shoulder. "It worked. I slept better than I have in...well, three years."

"Oh God." Relief flooded her system, and she blew out a breath. Her knees wobbled, and she covered her mouth to contain the choked sob that threatened to escape. Overcome by more gratitude than she had it in her to express, the tears fell and his tall form blurred before her.

"Hey." Voice soft, he pulled her hand away from her mouth, holding it in his as he stroked his thumb over her knuckles. "This is supposed to be good news, babe."

"You were late. You're never late. I thought..." She shook her head in helplessness, unable to finish the sentence. Her cheeks flamed. Only with Tyler was she this vulnerable, this exposed. She drew a shuddering breath, swiped at her eyes. "Never mind. It doesn't matter. You're here."

"Sorry, baby. I had something I wanted to finish before I came over and it took a little longer than expected." He cupped her face in the warmth of his palms, stood for a moment, stroking her cheeks with his thumbs. "I have more to show you. Is that okay?"

When she nodded, he took her hand again and led her back to the bedroom. Once inside, he moved to stand behind her and settled his hands on her hips.

"First thing is that speaker system by your bed." He held

an arm out, pointing. "I've downloaded all kinds of ambience albums onto my phone, everything from ocean waves to the tropical rain forest to instrumental music. I find I like the sound of rain. It reminds me of home, I guess.

"I also recall you waking me one night flipping on the light, so that was another suggestion my therapist gave me. To put in track lighting, something aimed at the bed, that you can turn on with a remote."

She nodded. "I'll call someone tomorrow."

He laughed softly. "Just like that?"

She peered over her shoulder at him, so he'd know she meant every word. "You're here, Ty. That's all that matters."

He kissed her cheek, then drew a breath and went on.

"There's more. The watch I showed you also has Bluetooth capabilities. You can download apps that will monitor your heart rate and announce it, sounding an alarm when you've reached your target. There are also fancier gadgets for the bed. There's one intended for epilepsy patients that will sound an alarm when you begin to move too much. And"—he ducked his head, resting his cheek against hers, and lowered his voice—"I've also spoken to my therapist about us. He's willing to see us both for a while, to teach us. I have an appointment next Thursday. It would mean a lot to me if you'd come with me."

By the time he was done, she was trembling so much she didn't know how her knees even held her up. She'd spent the last week thinking she'd lost him, that she was going to have to learn to live without him a second time. To find out he'd spent the time researching ways to not only help himself but them, too, was…overwhelming.

He wrapped his arms around her waist and drew her gently back into him. "Baby, say something."

Tears welled in her eyes all over again and a thick lump formed in her throat. What could she say? She wasn't sure she had the words. "You did all that…for *me*?"

"You're my world and everything in it. I spent three years thinking I'd never see you again. Damned if I'm going to just roll over and die. So I started by finding someone to help me. I'm better prepared now, and I'm not giving up without a fight."

Cassie turned in his arms and laid her trembling hands against his chest, needing the feel of him, his warmth and solidity, to ground her. It was her turn now. Over the last week, she'd done a lot of thinking, too. "I have something I want to tell you, too. Now might not be the right time, so don't feel pressured into answering, okay? But I have to say the words, because I need you to know where I stand."

He drew his shoulders back, as if preparing for bad news or a fight, and nodded. "All right."

Cassie swallowed hard. She'd rehearsed what she wanted to say so many times she ought to be able to say the words in her sleep, but staring into those blue eyes, her throat closed. Her hands shook so bad she was glad she wasn't holding anything, because she'd have dropped it. God, was this how it was for him years ago? Her heart clenched. He'd put his heart on the line, and she'd tossed it away, flung it back in his face like his words meant nothing. Like *he'd* meant nothing.

"I love you, Tyler. You are..." The words she'd spent hours practicing flitted from her grasp, blown away as if on a breeze, and Cassie closed her eyes, drew a deep breath and counted to ten.

It didn't help. She couldn't stop trembling, and the words were elusive bastards, deserting her when she needed them most.

With a sigh, she opened her eyes, ready to admit she was so nervous she couldn't remember what she'd wanted to say, except her gaze landed on his. The anxiousness in his eyes grounded her. Tyler wasn't just the love of her life. He was her home base. If she'd ever believed in the notion of soul mates, she was pretty sure he was it, because her life didn't make sense without him.

Calmer, she took a step closer, until the only thing she could see were his eyes, and spoke from the heart. "You're the reason I breathe, Ty. You're the reason I wake up every day, glad to be alive. The reason I smile. For three years, I haven't done any of that. So if it means we have to get two beds and sleep separate for a while, or I have to learn to sleep with the lights and the radio on, or even if I have to watch you go overseas again, I don't care. As long as—"

"I'm not going." Tyler shoved his free hand into his pocket, his shoulders bunching, and dropped his gaze to the floor, shifting his feet. "I've decided not to reenlist. I told my CO I'd give him any intel I have. The families of the soldiers who died deserve to have closure. But I don't want anything to do with it. They gave me honorable medical discharge."

She furrowed her brow. "Why?"

He shrugged but didn't look up. "Because the thought of going over there again, seeing that place, makes me sick to my stomach. I don't want to remember anymore. I just want my life back. They took everything from me, including three years I can't get back. I'm not going to waste one more second on them."

He finally looked up, his expression somber. His gaze settled on hers, intense and focused, like he waited for her reaction. The question was, what did he expect her to say? She was freaking thrilled. She wanted to jump on top of him and squeal. None of which she could or ought to do yet. She needed to take this slowly. For him.

She only knew his admission made what she'd planned to say next feel that much more important. So she drew a deep breath and continued.

"Well, I have to admit I'm glad to hear you say that, because the thought of losing you makes my chest hurt. Living without you isn't a possibility for me. Not anymore." God, here went nothing. She slid her hands around his rib cage and up his back, pressing closer. "Marry me, Tyler."

Long moments passed in aching silence. Tyler stared at her, eyes once again wide and stunned. Cassie's heart shot up into her throat. Would he turn her down?

His façade cracked, though, a slow grin curling across his mouth, and his eyes filled with amusement, with heat and tenderness. "Well, look at you. We have really have come full circle, huh? You know, princess"—he tugged her the tiniest bit closer and leaned down, his mouth hovering over hers, breath warm against her face—"that's supposed to be my line."

Her relief was so encompassing, so overwhelming, she wanted to weep. "I just wanted you to know. I want you. All of you. Forever. I want to wake up and find you in my kitchen every morning, and I want a whole army of rug rats with your gorgeous blue eyes. I want it all. The good, the bad, and the ugly. But I learned one thing over the last three years."

He dropped his gaze, his warm hands sliding over her back. "What's that?"

She smiled, his face blurring as her eyes misted. "I don't do so well without you."

He flashed a tender smile, amusement illuminating his eyes. "That makes two of us."

She lifted a brow. "Is that a yes?"

He let out a quiet laugh and brushed a soft kiss across her mouth. "That's a yes."

The tears she'd barely held in check escaped, washing down her cheeks. She dropped her forehead to his chest, shaking with the profound relief flooding her system.

Tyler crushed her to him and bent his head, burying his face in her neck. His breath was warm on her skin, his voice a husky murmur. "I love you."

"I love you, too." She murmured the words into his chest but couldn't bring herself to let him go enough even to look up at him. "Don't ever let go, Ty. Don't ever let go."

His lips brushed her neck, warm and soft. "Never again, baby. I promise."

Time passed in eons as they held each other, both of them shaking. Part of her still feared she'd open her eyes and he'd go *poof*, evaporate on the morning light. Like a dream. Tyler moved first, straightening and pulling back enough to meet her gaze.

"By the way…" He stuffed his hand into his right front pocket and came out with the ring, holding it between them. "I believe this belongs to you."

Cassie stared at the ring for a moment before looking up at him. "Are you sure?"

"Don't need it anymore. I have you." He flashed a soft smile and winked before turning his gaze to the ring. Frown lines formed around his mouth. "It's been sitting in my pocket for three years. I often slept with it clutched in my fist. So it's kind of a mess. It needs to be polished, but I'd like you to wear it…if you want."

The ring looked a bit like Tyler, a little rough around the edges, like it had been through hell and back. The gold band was now covered in hairline scratches that dulled the once brilliant gleam, and the small diamond had lost its luster.

"I want." Cassie smiled, her fingers trembling as she held out her left hand. "I don't want it polished, though. I like it exactly the way it is. Gives it character. It'll serve as a reminder of what we went through to get here. What *you* went through. I won't take you for granted ever again."

He slid it onto her finger, bent his head to kiss her hand, and closed his fingers around hers. "I have more good news. I got a job."

Cassie gasped and laid a hand on his chest, peering up at him. "Ty, that's wonderful. Where?"

"A bike repair shop over in Renton. I got a call from a couple of guys I served with. We got to talking while I was there. Jay called me a few hours ago. He said the background check came back great and I passed the drug test. I start Monday."

Cassie stared at him for a moment. He looked healthier than he had since he'd come home. He'd gained back some of the weight he'd lost and his skin had regained a healthy glow. Even the dark circles beneath his eyes weren't as pronounced as they'd been. Right then, he looked…happy. Her heart wanted to burst. "I'm so happy for you, Ty."

"The first steps into putting what happened behind me. Feels good." A sudden grin bloomed across his face, his eyes gleaming as if he had a secret. "There's more."

She smiled, heart light. "What's that?"

"I got the bike running. It's why I was late. Had a bit of trouble starting it the first time. It's downstairs, parked in front of the building." He bent down and brushed his nose against hers, his voice warm and husky between them. "Go for a ride with me, princess."

A heady shiver shot down her spine. She pressed herself into him, sliding her hands up his back. "I'd love nothing more."

Epilogue

Seated on the back deck of Grayson's houseboat, Cassie stared up at the darkening sky above her. For early July, the night air held a chill. The summer had yet to warm up, but the thick cloud cover had cleared enough to at least allow a peek here and there of the stars. All over the city around them, the evening filled with a cacophony of celebration. Laughter and the tangy aroma of cooking meat carried on the breeze. Pops and bangs rang out from all over, followed by bursts of color in the sky. Soon, the city would fire off a gorgeous display from the Space Needle.

She reached beside her, found Tyler's hand in his lap, and threaded her fingers through his. They'd been officially married for three months. Neither had wanted to wait but had agreed to keep the wedding small, friends and family only. Despite his misgivings, even her father had come. His presence had solidified the rightness of the day.

Tyler's therapy was working. He'd learned how to deal

with his PTSD, and she'd learned how better to help him. Slowly but surely, he was finding himself again, growing stronger. His nightmares had lessened, though his aversion to loud noises and crowded places hadn't changed.

Which was what worried her about his insistence on coming tonight. They'd be practically on top of the action.

She turned her head, peering at his profile. He had his head resting along the back of the wooden lounger he sat in, doing exactly what she'd been: staring up at the night sky. "You sure you're okay being here?"

It was the Fourth of July and Gray had invited the whole gang over for a barbeque. Not a mile from the Space Needle, Gray's houseboat on Lake Union would give them the perfect view. Cassie had originally turned him down, worried the whole evening would set Tyler on edge, but he'd insisted they come. Despite her fear, he seemed calm and serene. As if World War Three weren't going on all around them.

"For the thousandth time, I'm fine." He squeezed her fingers but didn't take his gaze from the sky. "I've actually been looking forward to this. I haven't seen one of these for over three years, and we met on the Fourth of July. Seems only fitting we watch it together. Besides, I have you to keep me grounded."

"Well, I won't let go of this hand." A huge explosion rocked the night, sending reds, whites, and blues streaking the sky, signaling the start of the city's display. She glanced back over her shoulder, through the open sliding glass doors behind her.

Sebastian, Christina, Cade, and Hannah were seated

around the small coffee table in the living room. Sebastian and Cade appeared to be having a serious discussion. Hannah and Christina had Hannah's eighteen-month-old daughter Emily between them. In the attached kitchen, some ten feet or so behind them, Maddie and Gray were uncorking the third bottle of wine. Or rather, Maddie was *trying* to uncork the bottle. With his arms around her and his mouth turned to her ear, Gray appeared more of a distraction.

Cassie cupped her hand over her mouth and called out, "Guys! It's starting!"

All heads turned in her direction. Christina smiled and nodded, then stood and turned to scoop up little Emily. Cassie couldn't help watching as Hannah got to her feet. Well into her pregnancy and due any day, she pushed off the couch hips first, her rounded belly jutting out in front of her. Cassie slid a hand over her own stomach. That would be her soon.

She turned back around to find Tyler watching her, a tender smile on his face. "Have you told them yet?"

Cassie turned her gaze to the water, her stomach tumbling with a sudden case of nerves. "No. It just makes it so real and honestly, the whole idea terrifies me. I mean, me? A mom? I don't even know how to cook."

They hadn't planned on getting pregnant, but hadn't exactly been too careful, either. In fact, she was pretty sure they'd conceived on their honeymoon and that there'd been copious amounts of alcohol involved. On top of the heady buzz that they were now married. He was hers, and she was his. Marriage hadn't changed the intensity of their need for each other. In fact, it had only seemed to increase it.

"You take care of me just fine. Besides, *I* can cook, and if it's a girl, she's going to love your closet." He leaned over and pecked her cheek, his voice warm and reassuring in her ear.

One by one, the gang all made their way to the back deck, pairing off around them. Hannah took a seat in another lounger on the other side of the doorway, Cade coming to stand beside her. Christina and Sebastian had little Emily between them, pointing at the various colorful bursts as they lit the sky.

Halfway through the fireworks, Grayson, standing with Maddie off to her left, nudged her with a hand. As she glanced up at him, mischief glinted in his eyes. "So. Got something to share with the rest of us?"

Cassie couldn't stop her mouth from dropping open. "How on earth did you know?"

He playfully rolled his eyes. "Please. You ate vegetables with dinner."

Cassie's face heated, but she couldn't contain her giggle. He had her there.

"Salad. I had salad. I actually like salad." Or at least, she would for the little bundle growing inside of her.

"No, you don't." Grayson laughed and nudged her again. "Out with it. We're all growing old here."

She glanced around at the faces of her friends, each one waiting with a gentle patience. "I'm pregnant."

Congratulations erupted around the group. Maddie

sprang forward, hugging her tightly. "Ooh, I'm so happy for you!"

Christina darted a nervous glance around, giggled, and covered her mouth, muttering behind her fingers, "I am too."

"Oh my God!" Cassie squealed, and launched out of her seat, rushing down the deck to Christina.

Christina enveloped her in a hug, whispering in her ear, "I'm terrified."

Cassie laughed as she pulled back. "Oh God, me too."

Hannah and Maddie joined the fray, hugging her and Christina from behind, and what began as a simple announcement quickly became a chatting frenzy. They spent several minutes sharing due dates and fears. As she listened to Hannah describe those first scary days of being a mom, Cassie glanced at Tyler. He was still seated in the lounger, watching her with that serene expression. Love shined in his eyes, calling to her like a beacon.

She made her excuses and left the group, sliding into his lap. He wrapped his arms around her and she snuggled into his neck. She hadn't a clue what kind of mother she'd make. She couldn't cook. Didn't clean. Hadn't no idea how to change a diaper. But she had these beautiful, generous people…and she had him.

"Aren't you the least bit nervous?" she asked.

"Not anymore." He pressed a tender kiss into her hair. "Whatever life throws at us, baby, we'll figure it out. Together."

Online, any fantasy is possible. But when virtual lovers decide to meet in real life, the temperature rises—and so do the stakes. See the next page for a preview of the first in JM Stewart's Seattle Bachelors series *Bidding on the Billionaire*.

Available now!

Chapter One

The musical ding of an incoming chat sounded through her laptop's speakers. Hannah Miller's heart stuttered. Standing in her kitchen, coffee cup in hand, electricity fizzled along her nerve endings, settling hot and luscious between her thighs. She didn't need to see them to know what they said. The same words popped up every night: *Hey baby. You there?*

Like every night, the same little flutter of excitement and arousal slid through her. Every inch of her came alive. He was early tonight. According to the clock on her cable box, it was ten past seven. They didn't usually meet until sometime around nine. She'd anticipated a couple of hours of waiting.

She bit her lower lip, gnashing it between her teeth. What she needed to do was wait before answering him. Keep him wondering. She didn't want to look too eager. Like she hadn't been biding her time waiting...in lingerie she'd bought just for him.

She glanced down at herself, fingering the hem of the pink negligee she'd donned an hour before. The sheer fabric fluttered over the tops of her thighs. It was the first time she'd ever splurged for something sexy, but on the way home from the bookshop this afternoon, she got to thinking about him and ended up in the Victoria's Secret on Pine Street. It was a spur-of-the-moment splurge. She'd taken one look at it and knew he'd love it.

She had to admit, wearing the see-through nightie filled her with a sense of feminine power. She *felt* sexy. Something she hadn't felt since long before her breakup with Dane a year and a half ago.

She sighed, set her cup on the counter, and gave in to the pull. Then she moved around the breakfast bar separating the kitchen from the living room and padded across the space. As she came to stand behind the couch, she rested her hands along the back and stared at the words on the screen. It had to be pathetic to look forward to a date with a man she'd never met. Night after night, she sat alone in front of her computer. The only sexual gratification she'd gotten in the last year and a half always happened solo.

She didn't even know the guy's real name. She'd been chatting with him for six months now. They'd met on a message board discussing a book, an erotic romance of all things. An easy friendship had developed that had become more over time. He made her laugh. He challenged her. And he made her see stars. She knew intimate things about this man.

Where he liked to be touched and how, what his kinks were, his hopes and dreams.

Yet all she knew about *him* was that he was Harley-riding lawyer from San Diego. They chatted via Gchat and both went by anonymous usernames. She was "JustAGurl456." He didn't offer his real name, and she didn't ask. He could be her neighbor for all she knew, the ugly guy in 45B who played the weird music at two in the morning.

Still, she looked forward to this part of her day, to coming home knowing he'd be there. Even if all they did was chat about their days, he was a lure she could never resist. More often than not, though, their conversations veered toward the hot and erotic. The man had magic fingers. He always knew the right thing to say to light her on fire, and those fingers always reached through the wires straight into her core.

She'd throbbed all day thinking about her chat with him. So much so she'd stopped on the way home for something sexy to describe to him. She only wished her lover could be there to see the nightie she'd bought for him. She'd even contemplated getting brave and sending him a picture or inviting him to a video chat on Skype. She'd grown tired of her own fingers. Even her high-end vibrator didn't cut it anymore. What she craved was touch and the warmth of skin. A flesh-and-blood lover.

Except she'd never been able to summon the courage to move beyond their anonymous chats. She had rules she'd lived by since her parents' deaths, since she ended up in a children's home and part of the foster care system. Inserted and forgotten. She'd set those rules aside for Dane. Since his exit from her life, she'd reaffirmed them. The top one? Never get attached. She was already growing attached to this one. The fact that she was here, waiting, proved it. She knew better.

Even knowing that, she moved around the couch and sat, picked up her laptop, and set it on her knees. As she punched in a reply, her hands trembled with nerves and the first stirrings of arousal. Yeah. This was why she was so damn addicted to him. Because all he had to do was pop up in her Gchat window and her panties dampened.

JustAGurl456: Hi. You're home early tonight. I didn't expect to see you until after nine.

bikerboy357: Meeting canceled last minute. Paperwork can wait. I had to talk to you. I've been looking forward to you all day.

JustAGurl456: Mmm. Me too.

Hannah inserted a finger into her mouth, biting down on the nonexistent nail. She shouldn't have told him that. Did she sound too desperate?

bikerboy357: Did you have a good day?

JustAGurl456: I had a long day. You?

Her day had been slow and boring. A couple of requests from her online bookstore had come in, people looking for original first copies, but the shop itself had been slow. Being in the middle of the rainy season for Seattle, the day had been dreary, the light drizzle enough to keep people indoors. Despite the shop sitting around the corner from Pike Place Market, only a handful of customers had come into the physical store.

**bikerboy357: I've had a helluva hard-on all day think-
ing about you. Made the day hella long. Let's do something crazy tonight, baby.**

That he'd been looking forward to her, too, had her insides clenching in anticipation. The mention of his cock
had fantasies filling her mind, and the desire to see him
flared to life in her chest. It wasn't the first time the urge
had hit. She had a million fantasies about what he looked
like. It was her favorite. She always imagined he had big
hands and a big cock. More than a time or two she'd
wanted to ask him to take a picture of it. She ached to have
him in front of her, to see the bulge in his slacks. She bet he
was long and thick, with a bulbous head she'd kill to wrap
her lips around.

Really, what she wanted, what she craved more than
chocolate…was his touch. To have him beside her. To bring
their online encounters into reality. She yearned for the
hands touching her to be his. To open her eyes after an intense, mind-blowing orgasm and find herself alone always
filled her with emptiness. She was tired of being alone.

JustAGurl456: OK. What do you have in mind?

**bikerboy357: Let me call you. I know we agreed to
keep this anonymous, but I'm dying to hear your voice.**

Her scintillating mood skidded to a halt. For a moment,
all she could do was blink at the screen. Call her? Was he serious? Her hands trembled again, this time from the nerves
currently wrapping themselves around her throat. Okay,
she'd admit it. She'd fantasized about talking to him on the
phone, actually getting to hear his voice. It would make him

seem a little closer, a little more human and not just words on a computer screen.

She'd told this man secrets she'd never told anyone, including her best friend, Maddie. Like how lonely she really was. It was something they shared. A love for reading…and a lonely emptiness nothing could fill. There were nights when they simply chatted, about life and horrible days and wishes and dreams. He'd become a friend, and she looked forward to their chats as much as she did nights like these when she craved his body the most.

She'd made her self-imposed rules to protect her heart. If one more person left her life, she might crawl up inside herself and never come out. Those rules, however, isolated her. The loneliness and monotony of her life got to her every once in a while. She longed to hear his voice, to hear the sounds he made when his orgasm ripped through him. Even to know the sound of his laugh.

Letting him call her, though, would take their exchanges to a level she didn't know if she was ready for. What did she know about this guy, really? Nothing. Well, okay, almost nothing. She knew his favorite color was blue, that he had a love for good Chinese, and that he was a reader, like her, but she couldn't pick him out of a lineup. She had no idea if he had siblings, or if he even had family at all. He was little more than a chat handle on the other side of her computer. One step above a fantasy. How did she know he hadn't lied about himself, the way she had?

Truth was, as lonely as it could get, she preferred their relationship this way. At least online, he wouldn't be able to see her. He wouldn't discover she'd lied about her looks. She didn't have long legs up to her ears or blond hair. She had mousy brown locks that frizzed when it got too hot and a short, plump stature. Maddie, her business partner and best friend, insisted on calling her *curvy*. But Hannah knew she had twenty pounds she couldn't lose for the life of her and that men tended to overlook her.

She also wouldn't have to watch the disgust wash across his expression when his gaze landed on the hideous scars cutting across her face. She wouldn't have to watch him stumble for an excuse, a reason why he needed to back out of an encounter with her. She'd heard the excuses one too many times. Maybe from jerks, but still. She didn't have it in her to start all over again.

Another message popped onto her screen.

bikerboy357: Hey, where'd you go?

With shaking fingers, she punched in a quick reply.

JustAGurl456: Sorry, I'm here. I have to admit, you caught me by surprise.

bikerboy357: I want to hear your voice, baby. I want to hear your breathing when you're pumping those fingers into yourself and what sounds you make when you come all over them. I want to know you're right there with me.

A hot little shudder ran the length of her spine, settling warm and luscious in all those places he mentioned. Her clit throbbed, begging her to take him up on his offer. She'd done safe for so long it had become habit, because the fear of history repeating itself froze her into inaction. Could she do this, though?

bikerboy357: Are you nervous?

She bit her lower lip, staring at his words on the screen. The answer came immediately. She shouldn't tell him, though. No, what she ought to do was stick to the script. So far she'd played fearless and flirty, everything she wasn't in real life. She enjoyed her online persona. For a while, she could be someone more exciting, instead of the book geek who hid in the shadows.

In real life, she owned a bookstore with her best friend, Madison O'Riley. They sold rare, hard-to-find books. Hannah was a geek. She'd survived her time growing up by sticking her nose in a book, by learning to keep her eyes open while blending in with her surroundings.

Truth was, she was scared of her shadow most of the time. When she became comfortable with someone, she could talk their ear off, but in real life, she was a wallflower. Online, she was safe, because nobody could see her. They couldn't reject her before they'd even gotten to know her, and she didn't have to worry about people leaving her life. If she admitted he terrified her, she might as well admit she'd lied about her persona, too, which would do nothing but change the entire dynamic of their relationship.

The word typed itself onto the screen anyway. She had to be honest or come up with a flimsy excuse, and she hated lying, especially to him. She might not be able to pick him from a lineup, but she knew one thing—he really was a nice guy, lonely like her, and lying to him made her feel too much like the very thing she loathed.

JustAGurl456: yes

Seconds passed. She bit down on her nail again, nervousness clutching at her stomach. Had she scared him off by being too honest?

bikerboy357: 312-555-1725. That's my cell number. How 'bout you call me then.

Her gaze shot to her phone, lying on the coffee table across from her. Its dark shape beckoned, daring her to pick it up. She swallowed hard. The thought of talking to him had become her latest fantasy. Getting to hear the sexy sound of his voice and the noises he made when he came. His breath sawing in and out as his arousal ramped up, as they pushed each other to the point of no return and he tipped over the edge with her. Yeah, she wanted that. Desperately.

Another message popped onto her screen.

bikerboy357: All right, honesty time? I'm dying to know the sound of your voice. It would make you feel not quite so far away. I hate that I can't see you or touch you. You're a big part of my day, but I don't even know what your laugh sounds like.

His admission tugged at the isolated place inside. She couldn't deny she yearned for the same things. Or that she'd had the very same thoughts.

Then and there the decision made itself, and she snatched her phone off the table. It didn't have to change things. He still wouldn't be able to see her.

Her fingers trembled as she punched in his number, and she hesitated at the last digit, her thumb hovering over the CALL button. She couldn't go back after this.

bikerboy357: I always imagined you'd have a sweet

voice. I can close my eyes and pretend you're here with me.

Oh God, that did it. It was like he'd snatched the thought right out of her head. Knowing he understood what it was to be lonely made talking to him irresistible. She swallowed down the fear and punched the CALL button before she lost the nerve. As the phone rang, her heart rate skyrocketed, a dull pulsing in her ears. She squeezed her eyes shut and took a deep breath in a desperate attempt not to sound as nervous as she felt. With any luck, her tongue wouldn't trip over itself.

Please, God, don't let me say something stupid.

The line rang once, then twice. Her breath stalled as she waited for the click, for a voice to sound on the other end of the line. Was he as nervous as she was?

"Hey."

His voice rumbled along the line, low and etched with a happy edge. Hot little shivers raced along the surface of her skin and a stupid smile stretched across her face. She'd thought of this moment a million times, and he fulfilled the fantasy. He had a sexy bedroom voice, deep and powerful but quiet, one she could envision listening to while lying in the dark. The thought of the naughty things he'd whisper in her ear had fire licking along every nerve ending.

She settled back on the couch and closed her eyes. "So why not find a real woman?"

"You're not real?"

His voice held an amused tease, and her pulse skipped. He had a sense of humor. A man with a sense of humor was sexy as hell.

"I'm a voice on the other end of the phone."

Another silence. This one longer.

"Actually, I consider you a friend. Someone I'd like to meet in real life. I've been thinking about that a lot lately. But to answer your question, it's…complicated."

The uneasy edge in his voice had her opening her eyes. She sat up, her heart skipping a panicky beat. "Complicated? You don't have a wife, do you? Be honest."

He laughed. The deep, sexy rumble had hot little waves rolling through her belly. "No. No wife, I promise. Just too much life. What's your name, sweetheart?"

Oh God. He had to ask her that. They'd agreed on this early on. For the sake of anonymity, she hadn't wanted to know his real name. That had to be pathetic. She had a lover whose name she didn't know and whose face she wouldn't recognize on the street if she passed him.

She drew a shaky breath and released it. She could do this. Hadn't she always wanted to move beyond her fear of being judged? She hadn't had a real date in over a year. The last one ended in disaster. The guy, a man she met on a match-matching website no less, had taken one look at her face and made excuses, like all the others.

She hadn't had sex for even longer, when her college sweetheart announced, out of the clear blue sky, that he'd fallen for someone else. She and Dane had met her first year in college. He was her first love, her first everything. She'd lost her virginity to him. They'd spent five years together, all through college and a year beyond. He dumped her a year ago when he announced he was getting married. Had cruelly pointed out his new fiancée was someone less encumbered and more exciting. He'd called her vanilla.

"I'd like a name to put to the voice. Truth is, as addicted as I am to our chats, I miss the human element. I've been dying to make you a little more real."

The hunger in his tone made her throb. She couldn't *not* answer him. This might be a fantasy, but it kept her going. She needed this. "H-Hannah. My name is Hannah."

He let out a quiet, thoughtful little "hmm." "That's a very sexy name. It's nice to meet you, Hannah. I'm Cade. Tell me about you, baby. What do you do? You never told me. You're always shrouded in mystery."

She settled deeper into the couch, letting the image of him wash over her and the husky timbre of his voice settle her nerves. "I don't want to talk. I want you to make me come. Tell me what you're wearing."

She didn't want to get to know him or consider him as anything more than what he was—some random guy whose hot voice and sexy words made her come so hard he often left her gasping for breath. Something she never achieved alone. Yes, she wanted more, but to give in to the urge was dangerous at best.

Cade *tsk*ed, low and amused. "You're always all business. Do you ever relax?"

"That's what you are. You're my vacation from life. Except I can't see you, so you're going to have to fill in the blanks for me."

"That can be arranged, you know. Us meeting, I mean. Tell me you haven't thought about it."

Her heart stalled. She touched the scar running down the side of her face. She had thought about it, a lot, but just the mention of meeting him in person had panic clawing its way through her chest and closing its icy hands around her throat. Envisioning his reaction, the disgust in his eyes when he looked at her…

She squeezed her eyes shut, her breathing coming harsh and shallow. He was ruining the moment, ruining her high by bringing reality into their exchange. He'd changed the rules, damn it.

She opened her eyes, desperate to drag this back to where it ought to be. "Are you hard, Cade? Is your cock in your hand yet? I bought lingerie for you today. A little see-through number. You can see my nipples. They're hard. Just for you."

He growled again, a muted sound that was half needy groan. The sound a man made when he was aroused and desperate for relief. "All right, I give. I'm hard as steel and you're the reason. And since you asked so nicely, I'm thinking about *you*. I want to know what you look like, every curve of your body. I want to be able to look into your eyes, know your smile. I yearn to know the feel of your skin. God, I bet it's so soft."

His words and the hunger within them shivered all the way down her spine, settling in a desperate place. Getting to hear him made breaking protocol worth every nervous heartbeat. She wanted to add to her fantasy, to ramp it up, so when she lay in the darkness of night, easing the ache by herself for the hundredth time, she wouldn't feel so alone.

She had another aspect to make her fantasy a little more tangible. She'd never admit it to him, but she yearned for the same thing. For him to be standing in front of her. To know the warmth of his skin, the softness of his mouth, and the strength of his embrace as he closed his arms around her.

She couldn't risk it, though. They had something good here. She craved more, the physical touch of his hands on her body, but hearing his voice would have to do because she wouldn't take the chance he'd end up like all the rest. She'd broken the rules with Dane and look where it got her. "Please don't make this difficult. This isn't what we agreed on."

He sighed heavily. "I'm sorry. I know it's not, but I'm addicted to you. God, I can't even tell you. I haven't had dinner yet, haven't even taken off my tie, but I had to talk to you. You're the first thing I want as soon as I get home. I'm hard all day because I look forward to talking to you at night. And up until tonight, I didn't even know your name. I don't know what you look like either, just what you've told me, and I crave it."

She closed her eyes and drew a shuddering breath. Knowing he looked forward to their chats as much as she did relaxed a knot in her stomach. Somehow, right then, it made him more than just a figment of her vivid imagination. She wanted to ask him, again, why he didn't find a flesh-and-blood woman, a one-night stand, but he continued before the words could leave her tongue.

"I'm going to be in Seattle next week. In fact, most of my clients are in Seattle. It's where my family's from. I grew up there. I go there a lot for business. The thought of being there and not getting to see you is driving me crazy. I've been back twice since we met, and every time I come, I have the same desire. To see you." He paused. "Have coffee with me. Only coffee. We can play it by ear from there. I have to see you, baby."

God, he had no idea how tempted she was. She couldn't deny she wanted the same thing. She'd thought of little else for weeks. What he looked like. The curve of his lips when he smiled and the broadness of his chest. How his hands would feel sliding over her skin.

It was long past time to distract him. "Take your cock out, Cade. Stroke it for me, long and slow."

Another moment of silence rose between them. Had she pushed too hard? Had she ruined the moment for him?

Finally he sighed, a sound of acquiescence.

"All right, baby. We'll play it your way. I'm too desperate to argue with you." The sound of a zipper being pulled down came over the line, whisper soft, and Cade released a ragged breath. "My cock's out. The sound of your voice has me so turned on. I'm stroking for you, long and slow, the way you like it. Tell me what you want me to do. I'm all yours."

Grateful for the change in subject, she closed her eyes and immersed herself in the sound of his voice, in the fantasy he represented. She slipped her hand into her panties and dipped her fingers inside herself. The sound of his voice turned her on as well. She was already wet, and her clit pulsed, sending a gratifying rush of delight when she caressed it with the tip of her thumb. "Tell me what you're thinking about while you stroke."

He let out a quiet, shuddering breath. "You. I'm wishing like hell this was your mouth wrapped around me. I'm imagining what you'd look like on your knees at my feet, looking up at me."

And just that easy, the desire flared like a glowing bonfire between them. It was the way it always was with him. So easy. They'd started out arguing opposite sides of the book they were reading. The attraction between them had grown as organically as the trees outside her apartment building. The sound of his voice had added a touch of reality and her body responded to the urgency in his.

She gasped as her mind took his hot image and ran with it. Her clit pulsed again in response to the images bombarding her thoughts. "God, I want that, too."

He grunted this time, a desperate, frustrated sound. "You're killing me, you know that? You have no idea how much I wish you were here. Slip your fingers into your pussy, baby. Be my hands. Tell me what you feel like."

She did as he asked, imagining him beside her, that her fingers were his. The sweet invasion had every sensitive nerve ending coming alive, and she gasped. "I'm so wet. You have me so turned on."

"You like hearing my voice." His held a hint of amusement.

She bit her lower lip. Her fingers stilled as her nerves rose again. Did she dare tell him the truth? Some part of her said she shouldn't, but the word left her mouth anyway. She never could resist telling him things she shouldn't. Like how much she wanted *him*. "Yes."

"Me too. You have the sexiest voice. Soft and sweet. I'm on the edge already. Have been all damn day, but your voice...God, your voice turns me on. Tell me what you'd do to me if I were there."

She swept her index finger over her clit. Her breathing ramped up a notch, coming in short rasps. Her mind filled with the images. Of him, seated on a couch, like her, his shirt open, tie crooked, pants unbuttoned. Oh yeah. She knew exactly what she'd do if she were there. "I want exactly that. I'd drop to my knees at your feet and suck your cock."

"You like that, baby?"

This time, his words came low and quiet. His voice had taken on an edge, and his breathing became a soft, erratic huff in her ear. It had her envisioning him closing his eyes, dropping his head back, losing himself in her voice as his hand stroked the length of his cock. The desperate edge in his voice made her wonder...was he as close to coming as she was? The thought only made her hotter.

She slid her fingers over her clit, circled, then down her slit and inside, working them in and out, imagining they were his instead. Every pump of her fingers tossed her closer and closer to the edge. Hearing his desire had ramped up her body's reaction. The fantasy filled her mind, of them watching each other, and had her orgasm hovering just beyond reach.

God, how was it possible to be this hot already, just from hearing his voice? "I'd love to suck you. I always imagined you were long and thick. Are you leaking? I'd lap it up with my tongue."

He drew a shuddering breath and let out a quiet curse. "God, I want you. I'm so damn close. The sound of your voice is making me crazy. I ache to be inside you. I want to fuck you until neither one of us can walk. Until you scream my name and come around me. You have me tied in knots, baby."

His words sent her over the edge. Her climax struck like a starburst, erupting through her. Colors exploded behind her eyelids. Muscles tightened and loosened, her heaving body clamping around her fingers as a rush of white-hot pleasure washed through her. She cried out, pumping her fingers harder in an attempt to make her orgasm last as long as possible.

Cade's groan echoed over the line, low and etched with the same desperation and intense satisfaction rushing through her. In a flash, the image filled her mind. His eyes squeezed shut, his fist pumping as jets of his come covered his chest and belly…

The image had another wave rushing over her, this one stronger than the last. Her body bowed off the couch. Her pussy clenched around her fingers, the intensity seeming to rip her apart at the seams.

When the wracking spasms subsided, she collapsed back into the couch, panting and spent. They sat in silence, only the sound of their combined breathing, harsh and erratic, between them. She wanted to thank him. She hadn't come that hard in…probably ever. It had been years at least since she'd last felt the sweet, sleepy lull of sexual satisfaction. The words, however, wouldn't leave her mouth. Exhaustion seeped over her limbs. Her eyelids drooped, her boneless body melting into the soft cushions.

"I have to see you, Hannah. That was incredible. Jesus, I think I saw stars. Think about what it would be like for real. My cock. My fingers. My mouth. On you. All over you. God, I'm hard again just thinking about it. We can make it happen. I'm going to be in Seattle for two weeks. Tell me you don't crave the real thing the way I do."

The desperation in his voice grabbed her, jerking her from the luscious lull of satiation. She couldn't deny she wanted the same thing. Lying there with her fingers still buried inside of herself, alone on her living room couch, the emptiness of her life settled over her. The way it always did when their exchanges ended.

She opened her eyes as the inherent intimacy of what they'd shared hit her full force, gripping her chest. Truth was, she wasn't a one-night-stand kind of girl. Deep down, she wanted a full relationship, and that part of her said he ought to be there beside her. Up until this point, their online affair had kept her going and eased the ache with little risk. Over the course of the last few minutes, however, it had lost its appeal. All because he'd broken protocol and had her call him. She'd heard his voice, had come so hard she lost her breath, and she craved more. Masturbating would never be the same. It would never again be enough.

She slipped her fingers from herself and sighed. "You're right. I need the real thing. I need *you*."

"Then meet me." Another plea filled with all the same hunger that had her shaking.

"But how do I know you aren't some weirdo who's going to kidnap me or kill me?" She shouldn't have asked him that. She should have turned him down flat and removed the unbearable temptation right then and there. Talking to him had always been easy. It was what pulled her to him and made him so damn terrifying at the same time.

He laughed. "You're right. It's a risk, I know. How about we meet in public? At the base of the Space Needle. I'll wear a red tie so you'll know it's me. That way, you can see me, but I can't see you. Then you can decide if you want me, too."

She was touched he'd go through so much trouble for her but reached up to touch the scar running from her temple to the corner of her chin. The night she'd gotten it came to mind. The darkened car, the twisted metal. Her parents died that night and her life changed. She'd gotten teased so much growing up that she'd come to expect it. Kids could be shallow and cruel, even in college. It didn't help that she'd gotten good grades and preferred her own company. She was a geek, a loner. She enjoyed reading. Her love for it had been what made her decide to use the meager inheritance her parents had left to open her bookstore.

Over the years, she'd been laughed at and discussed like she didn't exist, didn't have feelings. She'd overheard one too many dates in college, before she'd met Dane, talking to friends about the hideousness of her scar. Some had even laughed at her. Granted, they were drunken college boys too full of themselves, but the hurt had stuck. Since her breakup with Dane, she'd given up dating altogether. No, trying to find someone real, who'd accept her, scars and short, "voluptuous" stature and all, wasn't worth the headache.

She still had needs, though, and desires. She was twenty-five, single, and sexually frustrated. She had yet to have a wild fling for the hell of it. She lived like an old spinster, because she was afraid to live. She wanted and craved hot, heavy sex, the kind where you couldn't keep your hands off each other. Where you made out in elevators, like in the novel that brought her and Cade together in the first place. With a man, not the boys she managed to find. One who wouldn't be horrible behind her back or even to her face, who'd make her feel sexy while he fucked her into next week.

She wasn't, however, naïve. She knew better than to meet a complete stranger without knowing anything about him. "What's your last name?"

"So you can look me up? Smart girl. McKenzie. My full name is Caden Declan McKenzie, but most people call me Cade. I work for my father. Do a search on my name. I guarantee you'll find me. Now, you have to promise you aren't going to stalk me."

The playful tease in his tone had her imagining his smile, and the knot in her chest unraveled. She couldn't help a soft laugh. "I can guarantee I won't. It's not my style, but I guess you're going to have to trust me. Providing you are who you say you are, when would you like to meet?"

He was silent a moment. "You have a fantastic laugh, you know that? My flight lands Sunday night. Monday and Tuesday I'm booked solid. By the time I get back to my hotel at night, I won't be worth anything. Wednesday afternoon is free, though."

"I can do Wednesday. About three-ish?" She could pull J.J. in a couple hours early.

She and Maddie had hired J.J. a few months ago, needing someone to close the shop at night. Her little bookshop wasn't very big, little more than a small bedroom. When she'd opened it, though, she and Maddie had a dream, to do what they loved doing. Maddie was good with people. The shop had done better than either of them expected. It had grown steadily over the last three years.

Just recently, they'd lengthened their days at the request of more than a few customers, who couldn't make it in before the store closed at six. So, they kept it open until ten now. Last week, Hannah had covered her shift so J.J. could celebrate her first anniversary. Technically, that meant J.J. owed her one, though she knew the middle-aged woman wouldn't have a problem with returning the favor. It was why they'd hired her. She shared the same passion for books, and she had a sweet, need-to-please disposition. The customers loved her. This way, Hannah would have time to go home and decide what to wear before meeting Cade at the Space Needle.

"Three it is. See you Wednesday, Hannah."

The anticipation in his voice sent a shiver of the same trickling down her spine. "I look forward to it, Cade."

And did she. More than she probably ought to.

About the Author

JM Stewart is a coffee and chocolate addict who lives in the Pacific Northwest with her husband, two sons, and two very spoiled dogs. She's a hopeless romantic who believes everybody should have their happily-ever-after and has been devouring romance novels for as long as she can remember. Writing them has become her obsession.

Learn more at:
AuthorJMStewart.com
Facebook.com/AuthorJMStewart
Twitter: @JMStewartWriter

www.ingramcontent.com/pod-product-compliance
Ingram Content Group UK Ltd.
Pitfield, Milton Keynes, MK11 3LW, UK
UKHW022256280225
455674UK00001B/52